A ROGUE'S
LAMENT

Lilly A. Dreis

DEDICATION

"For my family, who, like me, had no clue how to do this; for giving me advice and helping me. For my friends who kept encouraging me. For you, who have gone back and forth on whether or not you can achieve your goal. You can and you will."

ABOUT THE AUTHOR

Lilly Dreis has always dreamed of being a writer. One day, she decided to stop waiting for tomorrow and become the writer she had always wanted to be. She has pursued writing ever since her parents first read to her. Lilly loves fantasy, movies, and stories of all kinds. She's a giant nerd who delights in strange facts and unusual words. She has won an Honorable Mention in the international *Writers of the Future* contest. When she's not writing, she's either lost in her daydreams or trying to wrangle her excitable poodle. Lilly Dreis currently lives in South Dakota with her family.

Table of Contents

"What lies behind us and what lies ahead of us are tiny matters compared to what lives within us."

-Henry David Thoreau.

"Only two things can reveal life's great secrets: suffering and love."

-Paulo Coelho

CHAPTER ONE

The land teemed with women. They lived without shelter, yet free from fear of predators. Clean water and food were never a concern. They had their own way of ensuring survival. *Manipulation,* they would call it, if asked. But they would reveal no more. Their knowledge had been handed down through generations, preserved quietly across centuries.

When Men arrived, the women decided to bind all their knowledge, guarding it in secrecy until the time was right to shift the tides. Yet nothing stays hidden forever. Whispers of the fabled *Book of Power* reached mortal ears, and soon, Men began seeking it, claiming it was for their king. So vowed the loyal and the deceitful alike.

The women cherished their knowledge: this manipulation of elements. With quiet fury, they concealed the book upon themselves, using both ancient wisdom and fresh anger to protect it. In the heart of the island, a vast forest rose, bordered only by rugged shore and steep cliffs. Still, the Men were not discouraged. They were not afraid or lost. They were relentless.

"Progress," they called it.

Upon the rocks, they began constructing a castle from the dazzling minerals they discovered. Enraged, the women summoned thick, brooding clouds to encircle the land. Torrential rains poured in a monsoon, halting the building for months. Violent waves crashed against the shore, making it nearly impossible for the king to reach them.

Eventually, a kingdom emerged. A village. Commerce. A society rooted at the inlet's edge. But no mortal dared enter the forest except the reckless few who believed in the book. They rarely returned, and when they did, they brought tales of wild maidens cloaked in bark, uttering words that sounded like nonsense but twisted the world around them.

Mortals gave them a name: *coven.*

The coven grew restless. With each intrusion and insult, their incantations became louder, harsher, more visceral. They fed their anger into the book, letting it soak in their grief, their pain, their resolve. Then the king issued a decree: an expedition was to retrieve the book.

"By any means necessary," he declared.

And so, the land and sky waged war for years. Both sides suffered staggering losses. The book was passed between the women, concealed on their bodies, its location ever-changing to keep it safe. Its cover, an animal hide, burned hot with their rage and turned icy cold with their vengeance.

They kept it for what was to come: the transformation of the island, the rise of *Sorcerac.*

They called it manipulation. Men called it magic.

"We only want to use its power to better the kingdom," they claimed.

Perhaps they believed it. But the women saw through them. They saw the lust for glory, for conquest, for domination, clear in their eyes even when they dared not raise them.

And the book, alive in its own quiet way, resented how it was treated. How it gave and gave, but never received.

Magic offered its silent bargain: it would grant you what you desired most, but in return, it would take something of its own choosing. The Book grew weary of its endless exploitation, passed between battles like a cursed relic. Its spells began to twist, hardening into incantations that no longer healed or protected, but wounded and tormented.

It was no longer revered. It became feared.

They began to call it *The Black Book.*

The witches, steeped in fury, carved spells into the flesh of their memories. With blood that pulsed with rage and sorrow, they inscribed their anguish into the pages. They kept the Book pressed against their chests, hidden from men who would twist its power for conquest. Yet in doing so, it absorbed their hatred and despair, feeding off their pain like a parasite.

It grew teeth in the wind. It found a voice. It created a monster.

And so the lament began, with the ocean licking the fractured hull of a ship grounded by fate. Foam bubbled up the ribs of the wreck like it were breathing its last. Only one set of footprints led away from the wreckage, vanishing into the mouth of a cave.

The rest of the crew was dead.

Igneus raised his eyebrows toward his captain. Romof stood silent, expression grim, pointing toward the darkened entrance. His snow-white hair and goatee only heightened the cruelty etched into his face. His scars flexed across his muscled arms as he gestured, taut and deliberate.

He pulled a long, curved knife from his belt, the blade unsticking his leather jerkin from the damp fabric of his trousers. The battalion moved lightly across the sand, their boots whispering into silence as they neared the cave. Though more had arrived as backup, none dared intervene. The law was clear: once a pact was made, no one else could interfere.

Igneus, clad in stolen chainmail draped over a grimy white tunic, his trousers stuffed into worn leather boots, stepped cautiously to the cave's edge. Inside, he spotted a man hunched on all fours, coughing seawater from his lungs.

The figure clutched his abdomen with one hand, the other arm sprawled beneath him, gashed, swollen, streaked with ruby and crusted blood. His coat was tattered and soaked in saltwater and gore. Long blond hair clung to his face like seaweed.

Igneus drew his dagger and pressed the tip just beneath the man's jaw.

"Killing innocents isn't exactly a pirate's goal, is it?" he hissed.

The man lifted his head, breath ragged. "Lad," he wheezed, "you clearly haven't met a pirate like me."

With a sudden jerk, the pirate twisted. From the captain's boot, he drew a hidden blade, slashing in front of him. Igneus ducked backward just in time. Romof let out a roar and lunged forward. The wounded man staggered, attempting a kick, but slipped in the water pooling beneath his feet.

Igneus lunged, tackling him. He wrapped his legs tight around the pirate's and raised the dagger, aiming for the throat.

"No. You. Don't," the pirate rasped.

He forced himself upright, slamming Igneus into the jagged cave wall. Igneus' skull cracked against stone. Lights exploded behind his eyes. Disoriented, he mumbled gibberish as the world tilted and pulsed.

A splash echoed across the chamber. Romof was charging.

He collided with the pirate, blade flashing. His knife dug deep into the already mutilated arm. The man screamed through clenched teeth, blood gushing over the slick cave floor.

Igneus blinked through the haze and saw it. A sword half-buried in a heap of abandoned treasure. Jewels and gold glinted like bait. His fingers crawled toward the hilt. Romof and the pirate wrestled beside him, crashing further into the cave.

Got it, he thought, closing his hand around the grip.

Romof wrestled with the dying man, trying to drive his knife into the pirate's chest. The two struggled, breathless and soaked in blood. Seizing the moment, Igneus craned his neck and sank his teeth into the man's ear. With a sharp yelp, the pirate recoiled from the cave wall just far enough.

Igneus, teeth gritted, hauled his new sword in a sweeping motion across the man's throat. Warm blood spilled over his hand. He let the body crumple to the cave floor, the sword still embedded in the now-silent pirate.

He stood there for a moment, catching his breath, staring down at the corpse.

"A pirate, huh?" he muttered over his shoulder, voice echoing in the chamber.

Romof approached, boots squelching through pooled water and blood. He looked down at the body with a cold eye.

"You remember the fire on the far edge of the village? That little houseboat?" he asked.

Igneus nodded. "Ten dead. Everything gone. This is that rat-king?"

Romof gave a grim nod. "Yes."

Without a word, he extended the sword to Igneus, now housed in a worn scabbard already cracking with rot. Igneus took it, then slid the blade free for a better look.

It gleamed. A silver edge sharp as if it had just left the forge. The hand guard curled like smoke, and the grip was wrapped in a thick leather that made Igneus wonder if it came from a crocodile or something more ancient.

He looked up at Romof.

"Why give this to me? This is a blood hoard. It reeks of death."

Romof placed a weathered hand on his shoulder, his grip firm but kind.

"Think of it as payment," he said. "You'll get your coin for this job, no doubt. But this... this is for your loyalty."

He paused, studying the younger man with something deeper in his gaze.

"You had a poor excuse for parents. And I never had a son. I never put much stock in fate, but..." His voice dropped. "Maybe it's trying to show me something."

Igneus was quiet for a moment, nodding slowly.

"I understand. How could I refuse that offer?" he said with a small, rare smile.

Romof chuckled, clapping his shoulder before turning to the militia assembling just beyond the cave mouth.

"What are we?" he bellowed.

"Judge, Council, Executioner!" they all cried in unison.

Romof gave one final glance back at Igneus, who remained still for a beat longer.

He approached the body one last time. The pirate's lifeless eyes stared skyward, open, blank, and accusing. Igneus carefully wiped his bloody hand on the man's tattered cloak. Then, kneeling, he reached out and gently closed the man's eyes.

"Whatever gods are listening," he whispered, "forgive him. And forgive me."

With that, he turned, sword in hand, and followed the others out of the cave. As sunlight flickered through the clearing storm, he slid the blade back into its scabbard.

And he walked toward whatever came next.

***

"Miriana, I have something for you," her uncle Igneus said as he stepped into his brother's tavern.

He crossed the room, boots echoing faintly on the wood floor, until he reached the far corner where she was sweeping. Miriana looked up, brushing a few strands of hair away from her face. A splattered birthmark ran over her left eye like a delicate smear of paint. She wore a long-sleeved blue shirt tucked into faded red trousers. Her raven-black hair was woven into a braid that fell like a rope down her back, curling slightly to rest atop her boots.

Everything about her set her apart. And she knew it.

Igneus handed her the sword without a word. The blade was long, its hilt silver and curving outward like crescent wings. The grip was wrapped in dark leather, and a pointed silver pommel gave it a final touch of elegance and danger. Miriana slid it free from its worn leather sheath and held it up to her face, studying her faint reflection in the gleaming metal.

From across the room, her other uncle, Valcom, frowned at the scene. His bright blond hair stood stiff in wild spikes, and his eyes, red-rimmed, tired, narrowed beneath deep purple bags. He wore a stained, tattered apron and maroon trousers, both crusted with years of spilled ale and regret.

Valcom stormed over and grabbed Igneus by the arm, pulling him aside.

"What the hell were you thinking?"

Igneus gave a casual shrug. "She should learn how to protect herself."

He turned to walk away, but Valcom yanked him back.

"She's a fifteen-year-old girl! What do you think people will say when they see her swinging that thing around?"

Igneus exhaled, eyes steady. "She's a fifteen-year-old girl who wears trousers in public. Whatever people might say, they're already saying it."

Valcom opened his mouth to argue again, but his eyes widened instead. He gasped.

"Don't do that! Be careful!" he shouted, darting back toward Miriana.

She had started testing the blade, swinging it through the air with surprising strength. The saber sliced just inches above Valcom's head as he ducked low, his hands scrambling to snatch it from her grip.

"I can teach her! I can teach her!" Igneus called out, hurrying to join them.

Miriana finally stilled, letting the tip of the sword rest on the tavern floor. She held it loosely, as if unsure whether to drop it or cradle it.

"Where did you get this?" she asked, her eyes bright with excitement.

Igneus smiled and gently took the blade from her hands.

Behind them, Valcom crossed his arms and rolled his eyes before turning toward the bar to begin preparations for the coming rush of customers.

"I have this job," Igneus began, "and it means I meet a lot of different people."

A snort came from Valcom's direction, but Igneus ignored him, only glancing back long enough to shoot a glare. He turned back to Miriana.

"Anyway, I got this sword from a pirate. Off the coast."

"A pirate?" Miriana's voice rose with wonder. "Seriously?"

"Seriously," Igneus replied with a grin. "Now, why don't you head out and go to the tree? We can start your training there."

Before he could finish his sentence, Miriana bolted for the door, the sword's scabbard clutched in both hands. The tavern door slammed behind her.

Igneus turned to his brother, pride written all over his face.

Valcom shook his head slowly. "You've got your work cut out for you."

"Let's go out to the tree," Igneus said, nodding toward the door.

With a tired sigh and a mutter under his breath, Valcom waved him out, grumbling with feigned annoyance.

Miriana paused just beyond the threshold, watching the two men. She knew something they didn't say aloud.

The tree was more than just a place to train. More than something to climb.

It stood on the very edge of the forest, just far enough from the village that most people stayed away. No one liked going near the woods, which made it the perfect place for a family that preferred not to be bothered.

She often heard her uncles arguing late into the night, their voices drifting through the walls of the back apartment where she slept. It was a familiar routine. That little room, once their youthful hideout, had apparently been their escape from adulthood's demands. According to Igneus, her father never had many responsibilities to begin with.

Miriana often wondered what those late-night conversations had been like: What they had laughed about, what they had fought over. Who was allowed into their little sanctuary, and who was left behind?

She pondered on these questions as they approached the tree the next day. The tree had grown taller than most in the region, its bark gnarled and its branches wide like open arms. Igneus stepped several feet ahead, turning his back to the great oak to face her.

Without a word, he reached into his cloak and snapped a dagger in her direction.

The dagger was barely a centimeter away from her skin when Miriana yelped and dove into the dirt, barely avoiding the gleaming blade.

"Never let your guard down," he said, already launching himself at her.

She rolled sideways, his body hitting the ground where she had just been. Springing up onto one knee, she awkwardly drew the sword from its cracked sheath. She raised the tip toward her uncle, now only a few feet away.

Igneus pivoted and swept his leg across the ground, his boot knocking against her blade and nearly ripping it from her grasp.

"I've been doing this a while, kid," he said as he straightened up. "It takes time. Practice. Discipline. You'll get there."

He widened his stance, ready again. "Try the offense."

Miriana lunged forward, swinging and parrying, pressing forward with effort.

"Very good. See? You're already improving," he said, stepping smoothly aside.

As she swiped again, she asked, "Is there a particular reason you decided to train me now?"

Igneus dropped to the ground and rolled, his feet kicking up a wave of dirt into her face.

"Not that I'm not excited," she coughed, stumbling back. "I *am* grateful. I know I'm more... manly than most of the girls I know. I just wonder. Why now?"

Igneus rose to his feet, hands raised in temporary surrender. "The world is changing," he said. "It's becoming stranger. More dangerous. I want you ready. I want you safe."

Miriana nodded, wiping dust from her eyes, and dropped into a crouch, blade extended in front of her like a question she was daring the world to answer.

Day after day, they met beneath the old family tree to train. As the months passed, Miriana grew taller, her limbs stronger, her swings more precise. Her uncles watched with quiet pride. She had begun training on her own, her motions sharper with each week.

Valcom, despite himself, occasionally peered through the tavern windows, feigning disinterest while trying to hide how impressed he was. Igneus, however, remained ever present, watching with a critical eye to ensure she never grew complacent.

"Again," he ordered one morning.

Miriana ducked, sweat dripping into her eyes. She had been practicing for hours. Her tunic clung to her skin, and her breath came heavy and shallow. Her form was slipping, her stance loose.

"Better," Igneus said just before his foot swung around and collided with her abdomen.

She hit the dirt with a grunt.

"But you left yourself open. And your balance is still off. Again."

"Break... please!" Miriana groaned, clutching her stomach.

"Again," Igneus repeated, now leaning against the tree, arms crossed.

With a strained breath, she extended her sword, stabbing weakly at the air.

"Once more."

A new voice cut into the moment. "Hello, all."

Miriana spun with instinct, her sword slicing through the air and halting just at the tip of Amalia's nose.

"Don't sneak up on me!" she snapped.

"You nearly cut my head off!" Amalia shouted back. "*I* should be the one mad!"

Behind her, Neel peeked out, eyes wide with fear.

Amalia ran her fingers nervously through her long, wavy chestnut hair, trying to calm herself. She wore a soft white dress that shifted into a blush-pink at the hem, like a petal glowing under sunlight. Her face was round and open, freckles dancing across her cheeks as her breathing slowed.

Neel stepped forward from behind her, brushing off his gravel-colored trousers. His dark brown tunic clung to his thin frame. Matching freckles stood out against his pale skin, and his spiky hair added a few inches to his height, at least in appearance.

He gave Miriana a wary smile. "You're not dangerous… are you?"

"Only to idiots," Miriana replied with a crooked grin.

Amalia huffed but smiled as well. "You two and your swords. One of these days, someone's going to lose a limb."

"Hopefully not mine," Neel muttered, taking another cautious step forward.

Miriana lowered her blade, her eyes flicking back to Igneus, who was watching silently from the tree with something unreadable in his expression.

And for a moment, everything was still again: the forest, the tree, and the wind that carried something old and waiting from beyond the edge of the woods.

"You must stay alert to everything around you, Miriana," Igneus chided, stepping away from his spot to greet the two newcomers. He grasped Neel's arm and pulled him in for a hug. After releasing him, he gave a brief nod to Amalia.

Turning to his niece, who was now resheathing her sword, Igneus approached with a small shake of his head.

He sighed. "Your enemies aren't going to cut you any slack."

Miriana groaned, sliding her back down the familiar tree until she was lying on the ground, arms cradling her stomach.

"Fine. Five minutes," Igneus sighed.

"No. Not five minutes. I have to be at the castle to work in the garden," she muttered, returning her sword to its scabbard. She began heading toward the tavern to stash it away, not wanting to startle any of the "normal" townsfolk.

"Yes," her uncle called after her as she and her friends took off running, "and I'm sure the fact that it's Tuesday has absolutely nothing to do with you leaving early!"

Miriana laughed as she sprinted alongside her friends.

"Are you heading to the wagon first, or coming with us to work?" Neel huffed, barely keeping pace.

"What do you think?" she shouted over her shoulder, darting into town. The grassy path gave way to cobblestone beneath her feet.

"I think it's ridiculous that you have to run across town just to reach the fields," Neel called out, finally coming to a stop.

"An adventure before work!" she cried joyfully from a distance.

"This is exactly why I said we should've just met her at the castle," Amalia scolded her brother as she slowed to a walk, watching Miriana pull farther ahead.

"I thought it would be nice to say hello," Neel said, a little defensively.

"Sure. That's the only reason…" Amalia raised an eyebrow. Her brother nudged her with a smirk.

"Stop making things up."

Miriana raced through the narrow streets, scanning for anything unusual. This was her daily routine before tending the royal gardens. She darted around wagon ruts, mud splashing up onto her legs, staining her pants and the hem of her shirt. Today, though, she had a specific wagon in mind—one she didn't want to miss. She had risen well before the roosters, just to be early enough.

The morning air was crisp, and for a moment, she could see her breath forming a faint cloud. She took a sharp turn, using her hand against a house wall to pivot. She nearly slipped in the mud, but caught herself, then sprinted toward the road leading out of the kingdom toward the expansive farmland of Sorcerac Island.

Up ahead, she spotted a bull-drawn cart. She ran to it, grabbed the wooden frame, and coasted behind it effortlessly, letting the bull do the work. Her face lit with joy as she tilted her head back to smile at the sky.

Peering ahead, she noticed another wagon stopped along the road. She released the cart and let herself slide to a stop before veering into the grass for better footing. She sprinted toward the second wagon, quickly closing the distance.

It was an old wooden wagon loaded with books, pulled by a sturdy brown horse that had stopped to drink from a muddy puddle. Miriana climbed into the back and began examining the books, scanning the titles and tucking her favorites into the crook of her arm.

Nearby, the owner of the cart was whistling and gently patting the horse's neck. When he turned and saw her, he shouted, "Hey!"

Miriana held up the book she was browsing, slid it under her arm, and bolted toward the nearby woods, careful not to drop any of her new treasures. The man gave chase, huffing as he ran, but Miriana zigzagged between trees, panting and grinning. Eventually, he fell behind.

Still running, the wind whipped across her face as she made for the glen she knew by heart. In the middle stood the ancient family oak. Reaching on tiptoes, she placed the books into the crook of its limbs one by one, then hoisted herself onto a low branch and carefully moved them aside.

Behind them, she had hidden a change of clothes; garments more suitable for a young woman of her time, and more appropriate for royal service. She slipped out of her muddy clothes and into a simple dirt-brown dress, adjusting it while perched in the tree. Then she traded her boots for a pair of light, soft-soled slip-on shoes.

Sliding down from the tree, she made sure her belongings were securely tucked away, then took off running toward town, bunching her skirts up in her hands. The castle loomed in the distance, towering above the patchwork village.

No one quite remembered how Sorcerac came to be inhabited. Its history had vanished with the ancestors, lost to the stars. The village bore the weight of age, its buildings stained with mold, their wooden rooftops patched like worn trousers.

The castle, in contrast, was majestic. Built from pale marble and sand, its origins a mystery, it perched along the coast, gazing out at the sea. The sky above was overcast, the waves below mirroring the clouds, each crest of water crashing like thunder.

Miriana took the long way around. She wasn't in a rush to arrive. She dashed along the beach, scattering sand with her feet. Gulls soared into the air ahead of her, startled by her laughter. The salty wind curled around her cheeks, tickling her nose. Sand filled her shoes, but she didn't stop. Joy flooded her chest.

With a gleeful leap, she whooped and twirled in the spray, kicking up sand and spinning in wide circles, dancing beneath the stormy sky.

All the houses and shops perched on the crests and uplands slowly came to life. Shutters creaked open, doors swung wide, and curious eyes peered out. People watched in bemused fascination as the young woman with the striking mulberry birthmark over one eye ran wild like a fish out of water. Her joy, though contagious, stood out like a splash of color in the sleepy morning.

Miriana ignored the stares, charging up the rocky incline toward the castle. Her foot caught on a jagged stone, and her slip-shoe snagged. She stumbled forward, cursed under her breath, then picked herself up and kept moving.

The castle's wooden gates loomed ahead, weathered by salt air and streaked with green algae from years of coastal mist. She gave the guards a cheeky bow, more mockery than respect. They rolled their eyes and stepped aside, letting her pass. After all, she was expected, though no one could say they looked forward to her arrival.

She loathed the job. Not the garden itself, but the people she had to endure. All but two.

"About time you showed up!" Neel called, smacking her on the back as she crossed through the gate.

He stood beside Amalia, both already dressed for work. Neel had swapped into a brown leather vest over his dark shirt, his trousers stained from the field. Amalia was adjusting her dress and brushing strands of hair from her face, her usual poised demeanor already at odds with the long day ahead.

Miriana grinned. "Had to pick up some books."

The three of them walked together toward the main castle steps, laughter and conversation filling the short journey. Tales of minor mischief and half-remembered stories passed between them like shared bread. They hadn't been together in days, and it showed in their ease, in their rhythm.

At the castle, they parted ways to receive their assignments, but not before making plans.

"Uncle's tavern after work?" Miriana asked.

They both nodded without hesitation. The spring solstice was always worth celebrating.

Miriana made her way to the garden at the rear of the castle, a sprawling patch of greenery often mistaken for a small park. As she arrived, she spotted Cecil, the king's steward, already fussing about. She stuck her tongue out at him from across the lawn.

Cecil noticed and immediately began ranting about "decorum" and "dignity." His voice carried like a squawking hen. Miriana didn't bother listening. She headed straight for the flower beds, crouched down, and plunged her hands into the cool soil.

This was the only part of the job she enjoyed, the earth. The scent of it. The way it clung to her skin. She pulled up weeds methodically, her fingers coated in dirt. It grounded her in a way nothing else did.

She reached for a prickly root nestled near the bushes when something soft and damp dropped onto the back of her hand.

Miriana screamed and froze in place, her whole body going rigid.

"Someone help! Swat it! Kill it!" she shrieked, refusing to move.

A nearby gardener strolled over, clearly unimpressed. He leaned in to inspect.

"It's just a caterpillar," he said dryly.

Miriana gaped. "What?"

"It's a caterpillar. Not a demon."

Miriana recoiled, voice rising in horror. "That's unnatural! Creatures should have *four legs at most*! More than that is an offense to nature!"

The gardener calmly picked up the wriggling creature and placed it gently on a nearby leaf. He gave her a long, disapproving stare before walking off.

Still unsettled, Miriana patted herself down, brushing at her arms, her neck, her hair, searching for any lingering horrors. Only after confirming she was clear did she exhale and return to her work.

Cecil hadn't left. He hovered behind her, still ranting about appropriate ladylike conduct. She tuned him out completely and made her way toward the old stone shed nestled beside the herb beds. It was where they kept all the gardening tools: rusted shovels, chipped trowels, and baskets that smelled of damp straw.

She reached the shed, tugged open the heavy wooden door, and stepped inside. The oddly familiar and comforting smell of soil and metal hit her instantly.

CHAPTER TWO

She deliberately pushed the door behind her, knowing full well it would slam into him. The wooden frame gave a sharp thud against resistance, but Cecil's reflexes were quicker than she anticipated. With one palm, he stopped the door from striking his face, the tendons in his wrist straining against the impact. His eyes rolled dramatically, as though the entire scene were beneath him, and with one long, commanding stride, he was suddenly behind her.

"You destitute little centipede! Look at your superior when he is speaking to you!" His croak was scratchy. His face bore the weary marks, creases that ran from nose to jaw, the heavy lines across his forehead. Yet his posture remained nearly immaculate, only a slight bend betraying the inevitable weight of years.

Cecil was nothing if not a perfectionist. His maroon overcoat gleamed as though polished that very morning, gold trimming catching what little light filtered into the shed. His brown trousers were pressed to a knife's edge, and even his buckle shoes, absurdly inappropriate for the muddy grounds, reflected a dull shine. He was a man who armored himself with presentation.

Miriana turned slowly to face him, her expression calm, though her fingers twitched as if resisting the urge to clench into fists.

"That's better," Cecil sneered, drawing himself up to his full height. He clicked his heels together with unnecessary flair. "I answer directly to the king, young lady. You would do well to treat me with respect."

Miriana's lips twitched into something that wasn't quite a smile. "I stuck my tongue out at you, Cecil, not the royal pair. So…" Her tone was light, dismissive, and she turned her back on him, stepping deeper into the shed.

The walls were lined with tools, neatly arranged in racks hammered into the old beams. She brushed her fingertips over a hammer, a sickle, before settling on a shovel. She pulled it down with deliberate slowness, letting the scrape of metal on wood punctuate the silence.

"You're a pompous, self-important fool who struts about as though you were royalty," she said over her shoulder.

Cecil gave a theatrical shudder, clutching his overcoat lapel as though her words were a dagger. "To insult me," he hissed, "is to insult the royal family itself."

"Case in point," she muttered. When she turned, he had already positioned himself in the doorway, barring her escape. His face glowed crimson, a ridiculous shade, as though he'd transformed into a human strawberry. His arms crossed tightly across his chest, his breath loud and shallow with indignation.

"You are nothing but a pathetic flesh bag," he spat. "You think you can challenge authority? You think the world bends to you because your drunkard uncles told you so? No wonder you grew up wild. No parents. No real family. Living in that decaying, rotting tavern."

Miriana's grip on the shovel handle tightened, the wood creaking faintly beneath her fingers. "That tavern means a lot to my family," she said evenly.

"Oh?" His eyebrows shot up with mock delight. "Did I strike a nerve? How curious! Such fierce loyalty to filth. What were they again? A slob at a bar and... ah, yes! What does the other one do? Lies? Cheats? Makes up tall tales to impress the drunkards?"

"That's enough," Miriana snapped, her voice cutting through the air like the crack of a whip. "Move aside. Let me out of the shed. Please." The last word was forced, bitter on her tongue.

Cecil tilted his head back and laughed, the sound brittle and cruel. He bent forward slightly, his laughter spilling into wheezing gasps. "Now you think manners will save you? Child, you are an orphan raised by two men who are nothing but friends with the dust. You are nobody."

Her knuckles turned bone-white. The shovel quivered in her grasp as rage thrummed through her veins. For one taut moment, she held herself back. Then the dam burst.

With a furious cry, Miriana hurled the shovel upward. The spade clanged as it embedded itself in the dirt just beyond Cecil's head. His eyes widened, tracking the weapon's arc, and in that sliver of distraction, she surged forward.

She shoved him hard. Cecil tumbled backward, his polished shoes skidding helplessly on the packed earth until his back slammed into the ground. She landed on his chest with a thud, knocking the breath from his lungs.

Her fists flew. One connected with the soft cartilage of his nose, a satisfying crunch beneath her knuckles. Again and again she struck, her fury unrelenting, until his yelps turned to pitiful cries. He clawed at her face, his nails scraping her cheek, but her grip was iron. Blood spilled freely from his nose, staining his teeth and pooling at the corner of his mouth.

Only when her arms began to ache and her breath came in ragged gasps did her punches slow.

And then she saw it.

Out of the corner of her eye, a shadow shifted. A servant had been standing just beyond the doorway, pale as a ghost. Their eyes widened in horror as they took in the scene. Cecil's battered, bleeding face beneath Miriana's fists. Without a word, they stumbled back, then turned and fled, their footsteps pounding toward the castle.

"Shit," Miriana hissed.

Panic surged through her. She scrambled to her feet, propping Cecil upright against the doorframe like a broken doll. His head lolled forward, blood dripping steadily onto his pristine coat. She wasted no more time. Sprinting out of the shed, she tore across the grass in pursuit of the retreating servant.

Her boots struck the flagstones as she slipped through the servants' door into the castle. Neel, polishing a candelabrum nearby, froze mid-motion, his brow furrowing as he caught sight of her wild expression.

Before she could explain, two guards rounded the corner. They seized her under the arms, lifting her clean off her feet. She twisted against their grip, but their armor made them immovable.

"Neel," she gasped, forcing a smile as though this were some harmless game. Her friend's face tightened with worry, but he said nothing.

The guards hauled her through the dim corridors. The rich rug beneath her dragged against her legs, the fibers scratching at the rips in her trousers. She caught her reflection briefly in a wall mirror: hair disheveled, shirt torn, dirt and blood streaking her skin.

They stopped at the end of the corridor before towering white doors. One guard rapped the silver knocker.

"Enter," came a strong, commanding voice.

The doors swung open, and Miriana was dragged inside.

The throne room loomed, vast and pristine, its vaulted ceiling supported by columns of marble veined with gold. She was thrust to her knees at the foot of the stairs.

Miriana bowed her head briefly, then raised it again with deliberate defiance. Her dress hung torn, streaked brown with mud. Her maroon trousers bore fresh blood. Hers, Cecil's, or both, she couldn't say.

The king and queen watched from above. Their expressions blended distaste with mild alarm, as though they had discovered vermin in their immaculate chamber.

King Cedric's rectangular face was stern, framed by a salt-and-pepper beard. His purple robe and fur-lined cape were disheveled, his crown crooked atop golden curls.

Queen Vivian, by contrast, was elegance embodied. Her emerald dress shimmered under the candlelight, though her bouncy blonde-silver hair failed to mask the dark circles beneath her eyes. Recognition flickered briefly across her features as she studied Miriana, but she quickly veiled it with composure.

"You called for me, your lordships?" Miriana's tone was mock-sweet, her smile taunting.

The king's eyebrow arched. "Child," he said coldly, "you stand before the law of the land. That insolent voice of yours may yet be punished. Mend your childish behavior, or it will be broken for you." His icy gaze pinned her, sending a chill through her veins.

Queen Vivian leaned forward slightly, her words gentle yet edged. "When meeting royalty, do you not believe one ought to take pride in their appearance?"

Her turquoise ring caught the light as she adjusted her tiara, and Miriana's eyes locked on the glint of gold in her curls, refusing to flinch.

"Your Majesty," Miriana began, her voice softer now, though the defiance in her eyes lingered. She bowed low over her knee, the torn fabric of her trousers grazing the polished marble. "Please forgive me. I was told to bring it urgently to this meeting and had no time to change my wear."

The king leaned back in his throne, one brow rising, before his gaze slid toward his wife. His lips twisted.

"Why are you dressed as a man?" His voice cut through the chamber, hard and suspicious. "Are you in league with the creatures of the wood?"

The accusation struck like a slap. Miriana's head snapped up, eyes wide. In an instant, the guards flanking the walls shifted, spears lifting with synchronized precision until their gleaming tips aimed directly at her chest. The sharp sound of metal sliding against leather echoed in the stillness.

Queen Vivian's eyebrow arched, the smallest flicker of curiosity in her otherwise measured face.

Miriana rose halfway to her feet, palms spread in pleading. "Your honors," she said, her words tumbling quickly, "I am a humble peasant who cannot afford much. My garb is purchased from the market. Dresses suitable enough to present myself before His and Her Majesty were far more costly than I could dream of affording. I beg your pardon for my crude dress and behavior. I am but a peasant. I know no better."

"Are you bleeding, servant?" The queen's voice trembled with practiced humility, though beneath it simmered her old resentment.

King Cedric leaned forward, studying her more closely. His eyes narrowed on the stains splattered across her shirt and trousers, the dark maroon patches dried to a rusty brown.

"Are you bleeding, servant?" he repeated. The question rumbled like thunder.

Miriana froze, her gaze lowering to her own stained clothes. She stepped back, as though distance itself could erase the evidence. "No," she answered simply. She offered no further detail, no crack in her façade.

The king's nostrils flared. "I grow tired of these games." His voice was low, dangerous. He rose from his throne with the weight of a mountain, purple robe spilling down the stairs, fur lining brushing against the marble. His golden crown caught the light as he gestured for the soldiers to lower their spears. "Whose blood do you wear, fool?"

Miriana swallowed hard. "Sire," she began carefully, "my duty is to toil in your Majesty's gardens, day after day. Today… there was a small altercation."

"A what kind of altercation?" Queen Vivian cut in sharply, her voice silken but edged like glass.

Cedric's eyes darted to her, irritation flashing. He mouthed for her silence, but she tilted her chin, unyielding.

Miriana exhaled, steadying herself. "One of your servants interfered with my work."

"How so?" the king demanded.

"I needed a shovel," Miriana explained, her tone crisp and matter-of-fact. "He would not let me leave. He blocked the shed's entrance. He thought it amusing to hinder me."

The king's voice thundered through the chamber. "And you killed him?"

Her eyes widened. "Oh no, your Majesty!" Her words tumbled out in a rush, hands raised. "I merely sought to perform my duty. When I reached for the shovel, he cornered me. He would not allow me to leave. I defended myself, nothing more."

For a moment, silence pressed heavily over the room. The king turned toward his queen, and between them stretched a wordless exchange. Glances sharp as blades, subtle gestures, a silent battle of wills. Then Cedric gave a curt nod.

"You may leave."

Miriana bowed low once more. She rose, gathering the tattered folds of her skirt, scratching idly at her leg beneath the fabric. The sound of her fingernails against her skin made the royal pair wrinkle their noses, scoffing at her peasant's impropriety.

As she turned to depart, her eyes caught the great gallery of paintings adorning the throne room walls. A cleaner was dusting a portrait of a long-dead royal, the golden frame glinting beneath candlelight. On a side table, smaller portraits stood arranged. Miriana lingered only a breath, then her hand darted out. She palmed one miniature portrait, slipping it deftly into the folds of her skirt. She smiled faintly, already imagining the coin it might fetch from an art critic.

Neel watched from across the chamber, pretending to polish a candlestick. His eyes followed Miriana with a mixture of worry and admiration as she strode toward the exit. She stopped in front of him and, with a smile, handed him the miniature portrait with a wink. When she disappeared from sight, he glanced down at the candlestick in his hand. The weight of temptation was irresistible.

He lifted the golden piece, examining the fine craftsmanship. When the coast seemed clear, he slipped it beneath his shirt. A hollow clang rang out as it slipped through and clattered onto the stone floor. Heart pounding, Neel darted his eyes about. The echo seemed to scream through the silent hall, yet no one turned. Hastily, he bent, scooped it up, and tried again. This time, he tucked the relic deep beneath his tunic, securing it against his chest.

He strode away with forced nonchalance, making his way toward the dining hall. His path led him through a corridor filled with sunlight, beams pouring through high windows. The golden rays caught on a figure ahead, and Neel's breath caught.

The princess was approaching.

Her blond hair shimmered in the light, a halo spun of gold and silk. She wore a gown of bright yellow, embroidered with delicate flowers climbing up her bodice and curling onto her sleeves. She laughed at something her lady-in-waiting, Amalia, had whispered, the sound light and musical, like a harp string plucked in joy.

He turned to leave but Neel's steps faltered when a voice, sweet and close, called from behind him.

"I believe that isn't yours."

He spun on his heel. Before him stood the princess in the yellow gown, her golden curls bouncing lightly about her shoulders, glittering in the sun. Behind her lingered his sister, her expression pinched into an annoyed smile, as though bracing herself for disaster.

Neel's grin spread wide as his surprise subsided. He slicked back his hair and bowed deeply.

"Good evening, your Majesty!" he declared in theatrical tones.

Princess Juliet's eyes widened at the boldness of the address. Amalia groaned softly, burying her flushed face in her hands, shaking her head as though to disown her brother entirely.

Neel bent lower still, his bow exaggerated, almost scraping the polished marble with his forehead. "Good evening," Juliet replied cautiously, one eyebrow arched. She gave the barest curtsy in return, subtle enough it might have gone unnoticed.

Straightening, Neel puffed out his chest. "My Majesty may call me whatever she wishes," he said brightly. "You are surely too busy to recall me, but if you wish, my true name is Neel. Should you ever choose to use it." He winked, as though sealing some unspoken pact.

Juliet recoiled slightly, taking a step back. Amalia muttered something under her breath, wishing the floor would open and swallow her whole.

"You may also," Neel added grandly, "call me your lover, if you so desire." He elbowed the princess lightly, as though they were childhood friends.

Juliet's cheeks flamed scarlet. Her fists clenched into the fabric of her gown, and her knuckles whitened.

Amalia, despite herself, snorted with laughter. Juliet kicked her sharply in the shin, forcing Amalia to drop her hands and choke back her giggles, though her eyes still danced with mirth.

Neel, oblivious, carried on with fervor. "Of course, you as royalty and I, a humble peasant, shall never be accepted in the eyes of your family." He raised the back of his hand to his forehead, feigning a tragic swoon.

Juliet bit her lip, the corners of her mouth twitching despite her best efforts to maintain composure. She bounced slightly on her toes, caught between indignation and amusement.

Amalia's gaze flicked between them, her grin widening at the ridiculous spectacle.

Neel struck his chest with a fist, his grin dazzling. "Fear not, beloved! I have a plan, so that I may rise like a prince and court you openly." He leaned close, lowering his voice conspiratorially, his breath brushing Juliet's ear.

"The most passionate romances," he whispered, "are always done in secret."

When he pulled back, his smile was broad and victorious, until he saw Juliet's face. Her eyes burned with resentment, and whatever playfulness had lingered moments before vanished.

Neel's grin reeled back in. He gave a nervous chuckle. Juliet responded by letting go of her skirt with one hand, balling it into a fist, and releasing it squarely into Neel's face. The sound of the punch cracked like a whip in the still room. Neel fell backwards with a groan, rolling onto the polished floor as a goose egg began to swell in the middle of his cheek.

Amalia let out a fit of laughter, clutching her sides as if she could not contain herself. Juliet shook out her stinging hand, waved off the pain, and turned to her lady with a sharp smile.

"Tell anyone I did that, and you and your brother will be in severe trouble," she said, her eyes flashing with both mischief and authority. Without waiting for a response, she turned back on her heel, leaving Neel sprawled on the floor.

Amalia's laughter slowed, and her expression sobered. She hurried over and crouched beside her brother, who was groaning dramatically as if he had been mortally wounded. She slipped her arms under his and tried to help him up, though he resisted at first, clearly milking the moment.

"Come along, Amy," the princess called over her shoulder, her voice clipped.

Amalia glanced between her superior and her brother, hesitation weighing on her. In the end, she hooked her arms under Neel's shoulders and hauled him upright.

"It's a fun little nickname," she explained hurriedly after seeing the frown on his face. She gave him a light shove to steady him before running to catch up with Juliet, her skirts fluttering behind her.

The princess looked back at Neel with a subtle eye roll that needed no words.

Neel brushed himself off, muttering under his breath with a huff. His cheek throbbed, but his lips tugged into a smirk. *Hard to get,* he thought smugly. He squared his shoulders, trying to ignore the ache, and slipped out of the room through the pristine white twin doors that led into the castle kitchens.

The kitchen was alive with bustling noise and extravagant preparations. Long tables stretched down the length of the hall, gleaming under lanternlight. Food was stacked high on shimmering china. Tables lined with towers of sugared fruits, steaming meats glistening with honey glaze, and loaves of golden bread still warm from the ovens. Wine poured endlessly into gold goblets, while pure silverware was wrapped carefully into satin napkins by quick servants.

Neel rubbed at his bruised face, the sting of the punch making him grin all the wider. His eyes darted greedily over the wealth laid out before him. Mischief lit up his features as he began his usual work.

He moved casually at first, waddling awkwardly as though the swelling in his face had thrown off his balance. He tried his hardest to appear normal, which only made him look suspicious. When no one seemed to be watching too closely, he began his art. With nimble hand, he swiped silver plates, tucked beneath his shirt like armor for his chest, silver spoons shoved into his sleeves like secret daggers, and forks lined against his legs like makeshift guards. Each piece clinked softly as he moved, the weight of them making his steps uneven.

A small bag made from a silk napkin, one of several he had already stolen, soon held his favorite trophies: golden napkin holders. His grin widened as he tightened the bundle, eyes glowing at his growing hoard. For a moment, he almost tripped on a pedestal, nearly spilling his treasure across the polished floor. His heart jumped into his throat, but when no alarm was raised, he let out a shaky laugh.

Back in Princess Juliet's quarters, Amalia worked carefully at combing through the princess's long golden hair, marveling at the horsehair brush in her hands. The handle shimmered faintly, its silver filigree catching the candlelight. She longed to pocket it, but the risk of being caught was ever-present.

"Of all the selfish, inconsiderate, arrogant peasants, why did you have to be related to that fool!?" Juliet exclaimed suddenly, breaking Amalia's thoughts. Her voice rang sharp, laced with disdain. She pressed a flowery beeswax concoction onto her lips, giving them a glossy shine.

"Package deal," Amalia muttered under her breath, so low the princess barely heard. "Twins."

Juliet opened a small golden casing. Amalia's eyes locked instantly onto it. Inside, a dark powder glimmered. It was charcoal for the princess's eyelids. Juliet began applying it with practiced care, her reflection growing sharper and more regal in the mirror.

Amalia's brushing grew erratic, her desire for the brush warring with her restraint. The bristles snarled through the princess's hair, and Juliet shrieked as her scalp stung.

"Ow! Be more careful, Amy!" she snapped. She whirled around to glare, her eyes narrowed with irritation.

Amalia's cheeks flushed, and in her flustered hurry, she allowed the brush to slip from her hand, clattering onto the vanity. "Oops," she muttered, stooping quickly to grab it. As she did, she deftly slid the golden compact down the ruffled sleeve of her light pink dress. Her heart pounded in her ears, but her face remained calm.

The princess gave her a light slap on the hand, playful yet edged with warning. Amalia shook her hand, sighed, and picked the brush back up, returning to her task. Juliet's glare lingered for several long seconds before she turned back to the mirror, smoothing her gown in her lap. The throbbing in her scalp soon distracted her from noticing the missing compact.

A knock rang at the door. Juliet lifted her chin in a nod, allowing Amalia to scurry forward and open the grand milk-white door.

"Your Highness!" Amalia gasped, dropping into a low curtsy.

"Mother," Juliet said stiffly, rising from her vanity and curtsying in return.

The queen stood in the doorway looking tired, but raised her hand with graceful authority, lifting her daughter and lady-in-waiting from their bows with nothing more than a wave. "I came to see how you felt about the suitors you had met," Queen Vivian said smoothly, "and if any had particularly set your heart ablaze."

"Mother!" Juliet hissed, rushing to push her out into the corridor.

The queen lingered in the doorway, her gaze both weary and commanding. "Your father and I may not have the happiest marriage, but with it, I became queen, as you will too one day. You were born from this union, Juliet. I left behind my entire life, my mother, my beliefs, everything I thought I knew. All of it was wrong, all of it reshaped. You must find a good match, no matter how difficult."

Juliet kept her eyes down, refusing to meet her mother's piercing gaze.

"Please think on it," Queen Vivian said bitterly before sweeping away.

Juliet shut the door gently, her fingers trembling against the carved wood. "You are very fortunate," she murmured to Amalia, "not to have to worry about such things. I never see my father. At all. Yet he dictates my life."

"Careful, your majesty," Amalia warned softly. "It can be treasonous to speak so." She hesitated, then added, "Still, being taken care of with no problems seems… wondrous."

Juliet scoffed, her laugh sharp. "That is its own problem."

"I suppose," Amalia sighed, resuming her work.

"You have nothing," Juliet said suddenly, her nose tilted high. "How do you manage?"

Amalia bit back her first thought and rolled her eyes when Juliet wasn't looking. "I work for the royal family," she answered dejectedly.

"Yes, but if you didn't, what would you be doing? What control do you have?"

"I would be starving," Amalia said simply, her voice low, "and wishing I wasn't. There's no control for us. We make what fate we can, as if destiny already decided it for us."

Juliet huffed, crossing her arms over her chest like a child forced into shoes she hated.

"Where is this coming from, your highness?" Amalia asked cautiously.

Juliet straightened her posture but gave no reply.

Amalia set the brush down with a sigh. "Did you want anything new for your hair?"

The princess sat in silence so long that Amalia almost repeated her question. Finally, Juliet's voice emerged.

"A large bun, tied tightly at the back of my scalp," she whispered quietly.

In the mirror, her eyes were fierce, glinting with something unspoken.

Amalia gathered the golden strands into her hands and began twisting, setting the bun upon the crown of her head. With one hand holding it firmly, she reached into the vanity's light pink drawer and withdrew a comb. She slid it into the bun to hold it in place.

The golden comb gleamed in the candlelight, with a single red jewel at its center. Amalia's breath caught. It was so beautiful it seemed heaven-crafted.

And she could not stop staring. She practically drooled at it.

CHAPTER THREE

A man slipped through the castle gates with the ease of someone who had done it before. His dusty leathers bore the marks of long travel, and over his shoulders hung a dark green poncho, its folds carefully arranged to conceal the belt of knives resting against his hips. He kept his head low, following close behind one of the palace guards so that it appeared, at a glance, as though he belonged to the escort. Few paid any attention to him. Those who did only assumed he was some minor retainer trailing after his master. In this way, he passed unnoticed into the palace courtyard.

The courtyard spread wide and bright under the afternoon sun, banners of the royal house rippling in the cool sea breeze. Romof paused for a fraction of a heartbeat as his sharp eyes roamed the expanse. He measured the place the way a sailor measured the tide: noting the symmetry of the arched entrances, the positioning of guards, the placement of doors and staircases that might serve as exits, or obstacles, if the moment demanded escape. He could almost imagine the fight in his mind, counting which soldiers he would need to fell, which gates would open fastest.

The air itself carried the briny scent of the ocean into every stone corridor. He tasted salt on his lips. A sudden spray of wind made his eyes sting, and he wiped them roughly with the back of his hand. When his vision cleared, he caught sight of her.

She moved across the courtyard as though she was wrapped in a golden halo. A young woman, petite and graceful, her yellow gown bright against the gray stone walls. Her hair shimmered like beaten gold, long waves catching the sunlight until it seemed to rival the sun itself. Her skin was pale, smooth as milk, and her sharp, green eyes could cut sharper than any blade he carried. Upon her head rested a delicate golden tiara, a single opal gleaming in its center like captured drop of moonlight.

"Princess!" The word leapt from his lips before he could weigh the wisdom of it. Romof bowed low to the ground, one knee nearly grazing the flagstones.

The young woman halted a few feet away. Her eyes lit up with curiosity. With practiced elegance, she gathered her skirts between slender fingers, bent her knees, and curtsied deeply, lowering her chin until it brushed the hollow of her chest.

"Good evening, sir," she said. Her voice was a melody, soft yet sure, each syllable measured with the grace of a born royal. "I beg your pardon, but might I ask whom I am greeting this day?"

Romof blinked, caught off guard by the politeness in her tone. He straightened and let his eyes meet hers with respect.

"Your Majesty," he said, bowing once again, "forgive my boldness. I am but a humble fisherman, come to seek audience with the king regarding a matter that troubles our waters." He paused, then added with a flourish that felt half-practiced, half-true, "Romof Montague, at your service."

Her lips curved into a gentle smile, small but warm.

"I could take you to the throne room if you need help navigating to it."

He shook his head quickly, glancing toward the nearby guards whose attention lingered on them. "I would never presume to trouble the princess with so menial a task. A lowly peasant like myself can hardly demand the company of royalty."

But Juliet, though he had not spoken her name, he was certain it was she, tilted her head with a kind expression. "It is no trouble at all. All farmers, fishermen, and workers are the backbone of this kingdom. Without you, what would we eat? How would we prosper?"

Her sincerity startled him. Romof allowed himself a brief smile. "Then I thank you, Your Majesty. I shall follow where you lead."

She stepped lightly ahead of him, her skirts gliding over the stone like waves lapping the shore. He followed at a distance, his gaze mindful of the distance. Each window they passed, each corridor that branched away, he catalogued with a soldier's instinct. Yet his attention strayed often to the Princess's restless gaze. She glanced often toward the knights they passed, her eyes lingering on the flash of steel and the weight of armor.

"Surely you have your own guard to protect you, Highness?" Romof asked at last, noting the soldiers trailing them.

She turned her head slightly, offering a polite nod. "Of course. Yet I have always wondered…" She hesitated, cheeks warming, before pressing on. "How one learns the blade. I have always been intrigued by defense, skill, strategy—" Realizing her own boldness, she lowered her eyes. "Forgive me. It is not a lady's place to ponder such things."

"You need not apologize," Romof replied smoothly, seizing upon the spark in her words. "My own father trained me with the sword. If it is something you truly wish, I could teach you. Not enough to defy courtly expectations—but enough to defend yourself, should ever the need arise. Reflexes well-honed betray no secrets."

The princess halted suddenly in the middle of the corridor. Romof walked a few paces more before realizing and turning back. He let himself sink into the thick carpet beneath his boots. *I could get used to this,* he thought fleetingly.

Juliet's eyes, however, brimmed with unease. "You shouldn't say something so blasphemous," she whispered, glancing toward the passing guards.

Romof bowed again, lowering his voice. "My princess, it would be my honor. Meet me in the stables. Bring a trusted servant if you must, someone skilled at silence. Everyone deserves the right to defend themselves, don't you think?"

She chewed her lip, eyes flicking to the knights at the far end of the hall, then back to the stranger who stood before her with unwavering composure. Her hand lifted to her mouth, gnawing gently at a nail. "I would learn… sword fighting?" she asked softly, half disbelieving.

"As much or as little as you desire," Romof assured her. "And why wait? The lessons could begin tonight."

For a moment, only silence hung between them. Then Juliet drew a steadying breath. "Come. I'll show you the rest of the way."

***

At Valcom's tavern, the night beat with a rhythm of celebration. The solstice had drawn half the city into the square, and the tavern pulsed with their laughter. Music spilled from the open windows, fiddle and drum weaving together in raucous harmony. Lanterns swayed from beams overhead, their glow mingling with wreaths of flowers strung carelessly across the doorways. The air was thick with the smell of baking bread, salted meats, and spilled ale. Voices rose in drunken song, strangers clasping hands, stomping boots against the creaking floorboards.

Behind the counter, a man with unruly blond hair struggled to keep pace. He slid mugs down the polished wood with the precision of long practice, though sweat darkened his yellow tunic and left blotches on his trousers. His hands were busy pouring, passing, wiping, repeating. But his ears strained toward the voice of his brother.

That brother leaned lazily against the counter, his hair whitening with age, chain mail rusted from use. He looked every bit the weathered fighter he claimed to be as he bravely recounted the tale of his latest kill.

At the bar, their niece sat quietly. Her dark braid fell tight and heavy down her back, her opal eyes glinting beneath the shadow of a birthmark that speckled her cheek. She leaned close to two friends, a brother and sister, who bent eagerly toward her whispers. They focused intently, their matching green eyes concentrated, as though her secrets were worth more than gold.

The tavern roared around them, but no one noticed the hooded figure sliding silently through the crowd. The stranger moved past the niece and her companions. They drifted toward the brothers at the bar just as the tavern master reached for a fresh brew, extending it without question toward the dark-cloaked guest.

Neel and Amalia then made claim to the makeshift stage near the hearth. Two lutes slung across their shoulders, strings ringing brightly against the clamor of voices and clinking mugs. They were hardly professionals, but the crowd was swept up in the fever of the summer solstice. Amalia strummed a lively song, her voice carrying a bawdy drinking song that half the tavern attempted to join. Neel scattered and spilled ale everywhere as he leapt from table to table with theatrical flourishes.

The congregation cheered, swayed, and clapped. For the space of a song, tavern and taverners were united. Until Neel, spotting an opportunity, slid to a halt before a gaggle of young women. They sat in a corner booth, voices chirping about the warm weather and summer fields. Their conversation faltered when Neel plopped on the nearest bench, flashing his most confident grin.

"Ladies," he crooned in sing-song, balancing dangerously on the table's edge, "do you know the best thing about bards?"

The women glanced at one another, unimpressed. Silence weighed heavy until one finally sighed and asked, "What?"

Neel leaned forward, eyes glittering. "Why, their lips, of course. Smooth from sweet melodies, strong from the air they breathe into every tune." He finished with an exaggerated wink, bow, and a blown kiss for each in turn. "And now, who among you would care to make music with me?"

The table emptied in a flurry of skirts and scoffs. The women departed as one, their disdain sharper than any dagger. Neel, left with nothing but spilled ale, straightened with mock dignity.

"Perhaps you need new material," came a gentle voice behind him.

He turned to see Amalia, hands perched on her hips, eyebrows arched in that familiar *you-brought-this-on-yourself* expression.

"Give it a rest, please." He slumped into a chair, letting his lute clatter against the wood with a reverberating twang.

Amalia, weaving carefully through the press of drunks, slid into the seat beside him. She wrinkled her nose, trying to ignore the stench of vomit that lingered from some earlier mishap. "If you ever practiced class instead of theatrics, you'd have secured a courtship by now."

"Spare me," Neel muttered, collapsing deeper into his chair, chin nearly resting on his chest.

Raising his voice above the tavern's roar, he bellowed, "Tavern keep! A pint, if you please!"

From behind the counter, Valcom, the blond-haired barkeep, sweat clinging to his temples, shot him a withering look. "I've told you before, rapscallion. I won't hand mock courage to boys who think themselves men. And you know my name, so use it."

Laughter bubbled from nearby tables. Neel huffed, strumming a lazy chord on his lute to cover his embarrassment.

"Speaking of boys with no courtship," Amalia teased, resting her chin in her palms, her eyes dancing with amusement.

Neel snapped upright, desperate to divert the conversation. "I heard a new soldier's training at the castle," he blurted. "A stranger, strong as a bull. Saw him sparring just yesterday."

Amalia arched a brow. "Changing the subject, brother?"

Before Neel could answer, Miriana strode into view. She carried herself with a confidence that defied the mutters following her. Her hand scratched absentmindedly at the birthmark speckling her eye before dropping to rest on the hilt of her sword. Whispers about her manlike airs, her braids too severe, her tunic too plain, followed her. She ignored them all.

"Are you tormenting my uncle again?" she asked sharply.

Amalia opened her mouth to protest, but Neel, panicked, waved his hands in refusal. He shot up instead, finger jabbing dramatically toward Valcom.

"What sort of bar owner refuses a man a drink?"

"The responsible kind," Valcom called back dryly, "who doesn't serve liquor to *children*."

Neel's retort died on his lips as Amalia elbowed him in the ribs. "Enough," she hissed, then turned to Miriana. "So, did you find any spoils this time? Or are you here simply to brood with us?"

"Always reminding us of her superiority," Neel muttered under his breath, rubbing at his side.

Miriana smirked. She ignored him and dropped into the empty chair across from them and held out both hands. Ten fingers, ten rings. Gold, silver, some jeweled, some plain, all gleamed in the lantern light.

"This haul could buy a horse. Two, if I'm shrewd," she declared.

Her friends leaned forward, eyes wide, admiration flickering in their emerald gazes. Amalia, though intrigued, tilted her head suspiciously. "And you gathered all this… here?"

Miriana swatted Neel's reaching hand away, snorting. "Not from this lot. These came from the streets on my way over."

Before further questions could be asked, the tavern door swung wide. Igneus entered with his usual swagger and the same confident smile, as a cat among mice. The people in the room fell quiet, either in his respect or simple wariness. His eyes fell quickly on his niece and her companions.

Igneus sat down next to his niece, the group making room for him. Eyeing the distracted Neel, Igneus then turned to study Miriana. Leaning close, he whispered, "So… is this the one you're courting?"

Miriana's face turned scarlet. Words tumbled from her in a single incoherent string: "*NowearejustfriendsI'mtooyoungandnotinterested!*"

Igneus threw back his head and laughed, the sound booming above the music. "I jest, girl. I meant no harm."

Their exchange caught Amalia's attention, but her gaze drifted beyond them to where Neel, unable to sit still, had slipped away once again. He stood now near the hearth, speaking with a wide grin and wild gestures to a slim young woman with cropped auburn hair.

A loud and forced sudden burst of laughter left his throat. The woman frowned, then, with deliberate slowness, tipped her cup. The contents splashed across Neel's head, dark ale dripping down his tunic. Gasps and chuckles rippled through the crowd.

Igneus slammed his palm against the table, roaring with laughter until his shoulders shook. "Never mind, Miriana. I forbid you to ever pursue him!"

Miriana groaned, burying her face in her hands once more. "I never cared for him in the first place," she muttered, though no one seemed to hear above Igneus's mirth and the tavern's continuing chaos.

At the bar, Valcom tried once again to offer the hooded stranger a fresh drink. The first one he had served sat untouched, foam gone flat, and in this place that was a rare and unholy thing. With a forced cheer, he slid a new flagon across the counter.

The figure tilted their head, studying the mug with unsettling patience. Their hood bobbed slightly, shadows concealing the expression beneath. At last, they lifted the mug into pale, gloved hands. Relief flickered across Valcom's face, until the stranger tipped it sideways and poured the golden ale straight onto the floorboards.

The liquid splattered and, drop by drop, seeped into the cracks of the wood. Then, without hesitation, the stranger let the mug clatter from their grasp. It struck the ground with a hollow thud, the handle snapping against the dusty planks.

The tavern's music faltered mid-melody. Laughter dimmed, fiddles stumbled, and for a heartbeat the crowded room hung in silence. To waste drink so brazenly was no small offense—it was, to many, a mortal sin. In the church of cheer and comfort, a man who refused ale refused brotherhood.

Igneus, halfway through recounting a tale of blood and valor, froze mid-sentence. His eyes shifted to the cloaked figure. He set his mug down slowly, deliberately.

The hood dipped toward him. A voice, soft but commanding, slipped out. "Is there a place where we can speak privately?"

The brothers exchanged a glance. Valcom arched an eyebrow. Igneus groaned into his mug.

"There's a room in the back," Valcom said at last, jerking his chin toward the hallway. "You can take him there."

"Must we?" Igneus muttered, his voice half a moan, half a plea. "It's late. Can't this wait until morning?" He thrust his mug forward for a refill.

"Not everything waits," the stranger said. Their tone carried finality, like the closing of a coffin lid. Without another word, they turned and began drifting toward the back of the tavern, cloak trailing over the ale-slick floor.

Igneus sighed heavily, shot a look of irritation at his brother, and rose. "You'll ruin me yet," he grumbled, lifting his drink as though it could shield him from what waited. He followed the stranger down the narrow hall.

At the bar, Miriana had drawn closer, curiosity plain in her eyes. "Work stuff?" she asked flatly.

"Work stuff," Valcom confirmed, scrubbing a glass that never seemed to get clean.

Miriana crossed her arms, unimpressed. "I hate it. I've always hated it."

Valcom paused, then met her gaze. "He doesn't like it either, girl. But it puts food on the table, keeps the lights burning, keeps this place open. He's carried that burden since before you could walk."

"It's sick," Miriana muttered, her lips twisting.

Before Valcom could answer, Neel's hand snaked across the bar, fingers curling greedily toward a bottle. Faster than thought, Valcom snatched his wrist. His grip was iron, his eyes sharp. "Don't."

Neel winced. Valcom held him there a moment longer, then shook his head and released him. Neel pulled back, rubbing his wrist, cheeks hot with embarrassment.

Valcom returned to polishing the same glass, his voice steady. "Miriana, you know how it was for us. Childhood… nonexistent. We carved a life where there wasn't one. By finding the loopholes—"

"Or making them," she finished softly, a reluctant smile breaking through.

He chuckled despite himself. "Aye. Making them."

"We had best head to the castle," Miriana said, turning to her companions.

"Some would say that's deplorable too," Valcom teased.

"But not *as* bad," she replied firmly. She and her confidants moved toward the door.

Valcom couldn't resist calling after them, "Don't get caught."

Miriana flashed him a grin over her shoulder. "We never do."

In the back apartment, the air smelled of dust and damp wood. A cot sagged in the corner, its straw stuffing threatening to spill through the thin fabric. A crooked table wobbled at the center of the room, two mismatched chairs standing like sentries on either side. Light leaked in through a pair of shuttered windows, weak and narrow, painting stripes across the floor.

The cloaked stranger moved through the room deliberately, brushing the walls with gloved fingertips, pressing lightly against the boards. They studied every corner, every seam, as if expecting hidden doors or listening ears. Igneus leaned against the doorframe, arms crossed, his patience waning.

"Planning to tear the place down, or sit?" he muttered.

At last, the stranger settled into one of the chairs. Igneus took his ale and joined them with a grunt, though his eyes never left the figure. The silence stretched until the stranger reached into their cloak and produced a leather purse. It landed on the table with a soft, unmistakable jingle.

The lamplight caught the edge of the pouch. Igneus stared at it, then lifted his gaze. "All right," he said slowly, "who is it you want axed?" He raised his mug, drank deep.

He did not expect a reply that sent a chill down his spine. "The king. The queen. And whoever gets in your way."

Ale sprayed from Igneus's mouth, splattering across the table. He coughed, eyes wide, color draining from his cheeks. "What?"

The stranger brushed a drop of ale from their cloak with calm disdain. "Is that a problem?"

Igneus slammed his mug down, heart racing. "A problem? That's not just a problem, that's bloody treason. You want me dead. Or worse, you want my family hunted until the end of days. They'd never stop chasing us." He rubbed his forehead, suddenly wishing he'd drunk enough to be senseless.

The hood shifted lower, hiding the face completely. A pale, delicate hand reached up to tug the fabric tighter. "Then perhaps this will change your mind." Another pouch joined the first with a heavy clink.

Igneus stared at the gold. His mouth went dry. "You don't understand," he rasped. "This isn't some nobleman with debts. This isn't a rival merchant. This is the crown."

The stranger's hand dipped once more beneath the cloak. A third pouch landed on the table, the sound sharp as a hammer's strike. Without waiting for a response, they rose.

"I will return the day after tomorrow," the voice declared. "You will have an answer ready. May the gods guide you toward the *right* choice for everyone's sake. And yours."

The door creaked, then clicked shut. Igneus sat frozen, staring at the purses. His pulse thudded in his ears. He didn't know how long he sat before the hinges groaned again.

Valcom entered, wiping his hands on a rag, expression unreadable. He closed the door softly behind him and dropped into the chair opposite his brother. "I'm taking time away from making money," he said dryly, "so you'd best spill the bad news quick." Arms crossed, legs folded, he fixed his brother with a knowing smirk.

Igneus didn't answer. He hunched over his mug, staring into the dregs.

"Someone's probably robbing me blind while I sit here," Valcom went on. His eyes flicked to the table, to the three untouched pouches gleaming faintly in the lamplight. He frowned. "Well? Who is it this time?"

Igneus pushed back from the table, pacing, boots striking sharp against the floorboards.

"Igneus?" Valcom asked quietly. He stepped to the table, curiosity gnawing. He picked up one of the pouches, loosened the string, and poured the contents into his hand. Gold and silver coins spilled out, bright and heavy.

Valcom froze. His smirk faded. He looked up at his brother, who stood rigid, eyes averted, jaw clenched.

"Well," Valcom muttered at last, his voice caught between awe and dread, "whoever they are… they must be very important indeed."

"Valcom," Igneus groaned, dragging both hands through his tangled hair as though clawing at the very thoughts swarming inside his skull. His elbows rested on his knees, his body folding in on itself. The lamplight flickered across his tired face, deepening the hollows beneath his eyes.

"Who was that then? How bad are these people?" Valcom pressed, his voice sharper than intended. He leaned forward across the table, the worn wood groaning under his weight.

Igneus said nothing. He lowered his hands slowly until his palms covered his face, fingers trembling. A low, muffled moan escaped him, the sound of a man not just weary but cornered.

Valcom glanced toward the small heap of purses scattered across the table. The weight of them seemed almost to warp the surface. He pushed the coins back into their home, tying the leather shut with care. He laid the pouch neatly beside its sisters. Then he pulled a decaying chair away from the table and lowered himself into it with painstaking gentleness, as though the chair might splinter under a careless movement.

"Igneus," he began, voice measured, "I have never accepted your job. Never. But if it is so bad that it has made you this—" he gestured up and down at his brother's defeated figure, "—this sick, then maybe this is finally the way for you to get out of that rancid society."

Igneus lifted his head. His grimace was sharp, his lips thin, his jaw tight. He dropped his eyes to the battered table, picking idly at a strip of wood splintering from the edge.

"I am to murder the king and queen," he whispered. The words slithered into the room like poison, making the air heavier.

Valcom shot to his feet, his chair clattering to the floor behind him. "Surely you don't mean to go ahead with it?!"

Igneus stopped pacing and turned. His gaze fell on his younger brother, the one who had nothing but still clung stubbornly to love for family, for his tavern, for the few simple joys of life. Guilt swelled in Igneus' chest, mingling with shame, and unexpectedly, love.

"I'm more concerned," Igneus admitted, "with what happens if I don't go through with it."

The words hung between them. The brothers stared at one another, silence pressing down harder than any shout could.

Valcom was the first to move. He stepped forward and wrapped his arms around his older brother, pulling him in despite the rigid stiffness of Igneus' body. Igneus smelled the sweat, the sour tang of spilled ale soaked into his brother's shirt. But beneath it, honest cologne of hard work lingered.

"That settles it," Valcom murmured. "I'll help you go unrecognized for a time. Your group wouldn't allow your leave of absence, not without blood."

"Valcom," Igneus sighed, pulling away and setting his brother's chair upright. "Don't say you have to because you don't. We have enough."

"Brother." Valcom's tone hardened. He gestured toward the pile of purses glimmering under the lamplight. "The person who asks this of you is a person of power. Look at the coinage they've given us already. They've threatened everything I love. That means everything you love too."

Igneus' face seemed to sag under the weight of the words. In the fading light, his wrinkles cut deeper, the shadows turning his skin ashen. He looked older than his years, as though time had worn him down. For a fleeting moment, his body bowed forward as though surrendering to the weight of the world.

"I'm worried about you," Valcom said softly. He stepped toward his brother, but before he could close the distance, the tavern door slammed open.

"*Is* SOMEone *GOING TO POUR ME ale, please?*" a drunkard hollered, stumbling in with all the grace of a ship in a storm. His clothes bore more liquor than his stomach could possibly hold.

Valcom rolled his eyes, huffed a humorless laugh, and began herding the man back out into the street. "I'll be back," he called over his shoulder.

Igneus barely heard him. His gaze had settled on the purses again, and they seemed to look back at him with a looming look. Taking this job meant risking everything. Refusing it meant risking the same. Was there no choice that wasn't a noose? He dragged his fingernails absently across the scarred brand on his arm. His *so*-called *badge of honor,* the proof he had joined the Wings of Massacre. Gods, what a cruel joke. That decision had been a chain, not a crown.

The door creaked again. Valcom returned, dabbing his shirt with a damp rag. "Someone had a little too much," he muttered. He tugged the shirt over his head, exposing his scarred torso.

Igneus' eyes lingered on them. Wide, purple streaks ran across his brother's skin like grotesque stripes, pulled taut when he moved.

Valcom reached under his pillow, pulling out a cleaner shirt that was hardly clean. "I don't have a wardrobe or closet," he said with a shrug. "I'm a tavern keep."

Igneus slid his chair over so Valcom could sit beside him. His voice dropped to a whisper. "Do they ever bother you?"

Valcom had just placed the mildew-smelling fabric on his shoulders when he looked at his brother.

He paused, glancing down at his shirt as though his gaze could pierce through the fabric to the scars beneath. His fingers worried the hem.

"They make me feel stiff," he admitted, "and as if I am unchanged."

Igneus sighed heavily, cradling his head in his hands. The pressure behind his temples throbbed into a headache. Everything—coin, duty, blood, family—felt like a web he could not cut free from.

"But," Valcom added, his tone gentling, "I remind myself that my past isn't my future. My destiny is mine to carve. Whatever I face now only makes me stronger." He placed a hand on Igneus's shoulder and offered a faint smile. "You will make the right choice."

Igneus lifted his head. "What if I don't know what the right choice is? What it looks like?"

Valcom chuckled, tilting his head back. "You and the entire planet, brother."

The laugh, however, did not soothe. It only deepened the emptiness swelling in Igneus' chest.

"When in doubt," Valcom said more quietly, "think of how your choice will affect the futures of those you love."

Igneus leaned back, eyes narrowing. "I don't know how it will affect them," he said truthfully. He turned his chair to face Valcom fully.

Valcom's worry deepened. "You know what I would choose if it was me, right?"

"Of course. Your self-righteousness." Igneus' voice dripped with brooding sarcasm.

Valcom scoffed, rolling his eyes. "You could get a *real* job," he snapped suddenly. "Not this inane hobby where you play vigilante." He spun toward the door, slammed it shut behind him, and left.

The silence that followed was deafening.

Igneus slumped in his chair, muttering curses under his breath. He crossed one leg over the other, propped his chin on his hand. Restless energy surged through him. With a frustrated growl, he shoved himself upright and marched out after Valcom.

"You know," he shouted, pointing at his brother, "just because you were treated like shit doesn't mean you were the only one!"

Valcom's expression hardened.

"I agree, you had it bad," Igneus pressed, his voice shaking. "Being ignored, overlooked. But I— I had to chop timber, build fires, fix the house, stay outside in the cold winters at night. I was a child too!"

His voice cracked, thick with memories that still burned. "I took this job so we could actually afford things! So we could be out of Simon's shadow!"

Valcom's retort was a hiss, sharp as steel. "Oh, please. You joined that group because you wanted to play hero! Just like you wanted to that night."

Igneus' eyes flared, wild and wounded. His voice fell to a whisper. "That was not my fault. And you know it."

Valcom paced the length of the tavern with his arms crossed tight, his fingers tapping restlessly against his bicep. His steps echoed faintly in the empty hall, boots striking worn wood that creaked as if under the weight of his thoughts. At last, he spun sharply on his heel and faced his brother.

"Mother and father were never quite the same," he rambled on. The word slipped out of his mouth, as though they'd been haunting him for years.

Valcom's eyes unfocused, gazing into some memory no longer in the room with them. "At fifteen, I thought it was because Simon was their golden child. The eldest, the strongest, the handsomest. I thought he was everything we weren't."

"We were children, Valcom. We didn't know better." Igneus gave a faint, humorless laugh. "But they did treat him as such. No wonder we always thought that way."

Silence settled between them. For a few moments, it was only the distant rattle of mugs drying on the counter, the smell of ale lingering in the air, and the soft rasp of Valcom's breath.

Finally, Igneus said, almost tenderly, "You always tried to keep the peace. You'd wedge yourself between me and Simon before we tore each other apart."

Valcom chuckled despite himself. "Of course, if Simon ever tried, you'd beat him bloody."

"And then I'd be the one in trouble," Igneus replied, shaking his head at the memory. "Didn't matter who threw the first punch, I was always the one punished."

They laughed together, the sound brittle but real, until Valcom leaned forward, his face darkening again. "So… what are you going to do, Igneus?"

Igneus leaned back in his chair, hands gripping the frame, elbows hooked lazily over the back. His gaze hardened, but a strange flicker of hope sparked in his voice. "Romof and I—he's always respected me. Perhaps he'd listen. Perhaps there's still a chance."

He rose suddenly, almost startling himself with the urgency, and hurried out the tavern door. For the first time in days, something like purpose carried him forward.

The shoreline was alive with music and laughter when he arrived. Torches flickered in the dusk, their flames bending in the sea breeze. A circle of men and women drank, shouted, and sang, their voices mingling with the crash of waves. Coins clinked, blades flashed in mock contests, and pride swelled in every boast about their latest spoils.

Among them, towering as always, was Romof.

"Igneus!" Romof's booming voice cut through the din when he spotted him. A grin split his broad face, and he strode forward, arms flung wide. "Come, boy!" He clasped him in a crushing embrace.

Igneus endured it only a second before pulling away. His throat was dry. "I need to ask you something. It's… important."

"Igneus!" Romof waved him off, chuckling. "Bah! Tonight is for revelry. Whatever it is, it can wait until morning."

"No," Igneus pressed, voice tight. "It can't. I'll say it plain. Has anyone… decided not to go through with the deal?"

The laughter dimmed around them. A few heads turned.

Romof's smile faltered. "What?"

Igneus forced the words past his lips, though they tasted like iron. "I don't intend to go through with it. I won't kill the king and queen."

A hush fell. The music ceased, the circle of comrades stilled. Only the waves dared to make a sound.

Romof's eyes narrowed. His voice grew cold, stripped of the warmth it once held. "What? What do you mean, you don't intend to?"

"I've done reckless things, Romof. Gods know I've spilled more blood than I care to count. But this? This is madness. I won't do it."

"Insubordination!" Gasps rippled through the gathering. To raise a hand or voice against Romof was unthinkable.

Romof's brow lowered, his expression unreadable. "Igneus, you've never been one to need convincing. Don't start now."

"You're not hearing me," Igneus insisted. "I won't do it."

Romof stepped closer, slow, deliberate. "Son. You were branded. That brand is your oath, your vow. And vows are not broken." His voice dropped into a growl. "If you refuse… then we will provide incentive."

Igneus squared himself, meeting his mentor's gaze head-on. "And what in the hells does that mean?"

Romof leaned in until his breath touched Igneus' ear. His words slithered, poisonous. "That niece of yours. She's growing into quite a woman."

Rage consumed Igneus in an instant. He shoved Romof back with such force that men stumbled aside. His hand twitched toward the dagger at his belt.

"Don't ever speak of her again," he snarled.

"Insubordination. Gasps rippled through the gathering. To raise hand or voice against Romof was unthinkable.

Romof straightened, eyes glittering. "Insubordination. You forget yourself, boy. I am the master here. The clients demand satisfaction, and we deliver it. Always. Or else…"

He snatched the dagger from Igneus' belt with practiced ease and dragged the blade across his cheek. Blood welled and traced a crimson line down his jaw.

"…We make examples." Romof tossed the knife back. Igneus caught it, hand trembling with fury.

Romof turned to the others, raising his voice. "Stick to the brand, or face the price. An eye for an eye—ain't that right, boys?"

The gang roared their approval, laughter resuming as though nothing had passed. Romof leaned close one last time. "Don't fail us, Igneus. Or you'll learn just how far we'll go."

Later that night, Igneus slipped back into the tavern. The smell of soap and ale hit him as he entered. Valcom was wiping down tables, stacking chairs neatly against the walls. The day's noise was gone; only quiet lingered.

"I told them I wanted out," Igneus whispered.

"They didn't listen," Valcom muttered without looking up. His rag scraped harder against the wood, his jaw clenched tight.

"I don't know what else to do." Igneus said. "Think of Miriana."

Valcom's eyes flicked to him, then softened. "Always."

"Then you see. If I defy them, she's the one they'll hurt."

"Then leave. Don't do it—flee the island."

Igneus shook his head. "It's an island. They'd find me."

Valcom dropped the rag onto the counter and faced him fully, gesturing to his brother's face. "Then fight them. Better to bleed with honor than bow to cowards."

Igneus opened his mouth to answer, but the door creaked behind them. Both brothers turned sharply.

Miriana entered, hair loose around her shoulders, eyes weary but bright. "Everything all right?" she asked. "What happened to you?" she gestured to Igneus' cut.

"I could ask you the same," Valcom said.

"Work problems," Igneus cut in quickly. He thrust a broom at her. "Here. Help us close."

She took it, arching a brow. "Me too. Work problems, I mean." But she began to sweep.

Igneus drifted behind the counter. He busied himself scratching absently at his brand. His nails dug too deep; blood pricked through the scarred flesh before he noticed. His mind spun with thoughts of knives and oaths and chains he could not see but felt all the same.

"Igneus?" Miriana's voice broke through. She and Valcom were watching him, worry in their faces.

He forced a hollow chuckle. "Oh, you know. Trapped in old memories."

She turned back to sweeping, though slower now. The silence stretched until she spoke again.

"I used to wonder if my birthmark came from my mother or father." Her fingers brushed the dark stain across her eye. "But I know better now. I just… sometimes wonder if I look like them at all."

The brothers shifted uncomfortably, neither willing to answer.

"We never talk about them," she said, voice trembling. "Were they… were they as bad as—"

"*No,*" Igneus snapped too quickly. His hand tightened around a dagger, dragging it against a whetstone as though to drown her question in steel. "But they weren't saints either."

"Who abandons their two-week-old daughter?" he added bitterly.

"Igneus!" Valcom barked.

But Miriana only stepped closer, setting the broom aside. Her face was unreadable. "Don't I deserve to know?"

Neither uncle answered.

At last, Igneus exhaled, shoulders slumping. "Fine. Then listen, Miriana. Listen to the truth."

And he began to tell her the wounded memory.

***

64

Simon and his wife, Celeste, entered the molding tavern. This seemed normal enough, but if one looked closer, an onlooker may notice that the bundle of cloth the woman was holding, strangely contained a babe.

Valcom, who was a thin man with light blonde, almost white, hair, took notice of them behind the counter and leapt over it to greet them.

He began talking speedily and excitedly, the brightest smile coming over his face. He forgot all that had transpired between them. He was excited to meet his niece. Igneus, from the back of the tavern clad in chain mail, approached, grinning and opening his arms for an embrace, also happier than enraged at this greeting. The couple received them both warmly, but their faces were creased with concern. Valcom inquired about it, and the couple responded that they must take leave for a strange new land.

They said they wanted adventure, and a cursed child with a witch's mark would hold no future. So, why should the child stifle theirs? This saddened and upset the two men as they continuously gestured to the infant in their arms. The couple shook their heads.

"You're not understanding," they said. "We would be doing this for her."

"She should learn the truth soon enough," the thin man with the bright blonde hair growled and walked back towards his counter. The man in chain mail asked what was to become of the baby while they were away.

The uncles had hoped, perhaps naively, that the couple would reconsider and leave Miriana in their care only temporarily. True, the uncles had immediately loved the child, but their lives, their occupations, their world was hardly suited to an infant at that very moment. There were obligations that tied them down, work that demanded constant presence, tavern duties that left little room for midnight cries or lullabies. The chain-mailed man, Igneus, tried to convey this to the couple with firm reason, but Simon and Celeste were immovable.

The couple felt something—a pull, a tug inwards as though fate had drawn a map before their eyes. There was a direction calling to them, a land they swore could be their refuge, a place private and far away where no one would bother them. That conviction made Igneus bristle. His jaw tightened under his beard, and frustration colored his face. Finally, he could hold it no longer. He jabbed a finger sharply toward his brother Simon, who stood close with Celeste.

"You have everything," Igneus barked, voice cracking, "while your brothers scrape by with nothing. Is that not enough? Do you even see it? I would kill to have your life."

The last word broke out of him like a curse. His eyes burned, and hot tears began to slide unbidden down his weathered face. The tavern had grown quieter, a hush that prickled the air. Simon stepped forward, hand half-extended, trying to console him. But the gesture, however well-meaning, only deepened Igneus' hurt.

"Don't you pity me," Igneus snarled. He shoved Simon, the motion rough, desperate. His brother stumbled back into a table, and the crash made the few occupants grumble their disapproval. The scrape of chairs echoed as men turned their heads, frowning at the disruption. Simon straightened, his fury blazing, and met his brother's gaze with fire.

Anger overtook his senses and Simon hissed through clenched teeth, "You do kill—to pretend to have my life."

The words cut, sharp as any blade. Celeste gasped, clutching the baby tight to her chest. She seized her husband's arm, trying to anchor him back into reason, but it was pointless. His rage surged unchecked. With a violent shrug, he shoved Celeste aside. She stumbled and would have fallen had Valcom not darted forward, catching her firmly.

"Enough!" Valcom cried, but his plea dissolved in the air.

Simon lunged at Igneus, tackling him. The table splintered beneath the weight of their struggle, wood cracking and scattering tankards to the floor. Patrons cursed, chairs scraping as they scuttled away from the brawl. Igneus roared as Simon's arms clamped around his throat in a choking grip. With desperate instinct, Igneus ducked his chin to his chest, pinning Simon's finger painfully beneath it. He swung his fists blindly, knuckles cracking against Simon's cheek. Then, gathering all his strength, he thrust upward, jerking his body violently. The motion wrenched him free, and he rolled aside, coughing and clutching at his neck for breath.

For a moment, Igneus lay there, wheezing. His chest rose and fell like a bellows, breath rattling in his throat. Then a hand pressed down onto his shoulder. Simon. The touch was deceptively gentle, but Igneus' instincts flared. He twisted, driving his fist hard into his brother's face.

The blow snapped Simon's head back. He reeled, blood spilling from his nostrils like a river. He staggered into the path of departing patrons, almost colliding with them, but steadied himself quickly.

Wiping the crimson smear across the back of his hand, he let out a small, feral whimper, and then launched himself again.

They hit the ground hard, bodies rolling, fists flying. Simon pummeled Igneus' face, each strike fueled by years of rivalry, jealousy, and unspoken bitterness. Igneus grappled, shoving with all his strength, his older brother's hand grinding into his jaw.

Celeste cried out, panic in her voice. She thrust the baby into Valcom's arms and ran toward her husband, trying desperately to pull him off. "Simon! Stop! Please!"

But Simon only growled, feral, as if her voice couldn't reach him. He shoved her aside once more. Celeste tumbled, the crowd gasping. Valcom caught her again, firm but gentle, placing Miriana back into her arms as if nothing in the world mattered more than the child's safety. He guided her toward the bar, pulling out a chair with steady hands. His calmness in that chaos was eerie. He poured her a glass of water from a pitcher, pressing it into her trembling fingers before rising once again to face the storm between his brothers.

"Enough!" Valcom roared.

The sound startled even him. His voice, usually quiet and warm, cracked like thunder through the tavern. Simon and Igneus froze mid-grapple. It was so strange and so unnatural to see their youngest brother filled with such command that the room itself seemed to pause.

The tavern was silent. All eyes turned toward Valcom.

He swept his gaze around, jaw set, and when his eyes landed on the scattered patrons, they quickly ducked back to their cups, pretending nothing had happened. Slowly, carefully, Valcom lowered his hands, breathing hard.

"If you need to leave, fine," he said, his voice still sharp. "But if you go—'tavern-keep' over here is going to spend the most time with the kid."

The silence stretched. Then, without another word, he strode forward, plucked the child from Celeste's arms, and turned his back to them all. His shoulders were tense as he carried the babe toward the bar.

"Wait!" Celeste's voice broke, raw and pleading. She and Simon followed him, desperation carving their faces. "Please! You don't understand. We need to explain!"

The tankards lowered and whispers stirred as patrons leaned in with curiosity.

Valcom's voice shook as he asked, "What is the child's name?"

Celeste's lips trembled. "Miriana Fortis Ele."

The name hung in the air, heavy and solemn. Valcom blinked, the weight of it settling onto him.

"We need you to raise her," Celeste whispered. "We've decided to sail for new lands. She wouldn't be safe with us. The mark… it is a curse. You know what they said was here before…" Her voice dropped to a hushed, fearful whisper. "Witches."

Igneus let out a bitter cough of laughter. He tried to stifle it but couldn't. Valcom nearly rolled his eyes.

"Your father," Igneus said, voice thick with scorn, "believed the sea hid its fish from him and him alone."

"Or perhaps," Simon shot back, eyes narrowing, "it is recompense for my brother's wicked jobs."

Valcom bristled. His patience frayed thin.

"It's just a birthmark," he snapped. "It could be a blessing, too. Our parents were wicked, yes. If you want to believe in divine punishment, then place it on them, on their actions, not this child! She knows nothing of the history, nothing of the pain we've endured. You have a chance—" his voice became fierce with passion, "—a chance to make sure nothing like that ever touches her again!"

The tavern buzzed with unease. For a moment, all hung suspended between them, the curse, the baby, the brothers' battered pride.

And then, without warning, Valcom turned his back, Miriana cradled in his arms. He and Igneus shut the couple out with their silence and never looked for them again.

****

"That," Valcom muttered, more to himself than to anyone else, "was the last time I ever searched out your parents, child."

"Listen, kid—" Valcom began. But the words faltered as a shout cut him off.

"I said—" a man slammed his mug down with a thunderous boom. The sound jolted through the tavern, silencing the chatter once again. Valcom winced, sweat beading along his brow.

"I want another drink."

"I-I understand, fri—sir," Valcom stammered, "but I—I believe you should be done for tonight. For your health, sir."

The man's eyes narrowed. His voice turned to venom.

"That's not your job," he hissed. "You provide the drink. I drink. That's it. What happens after—" He leaned forward, breath hot and suffocating against Valcom's face, "—is not your concern."

"Listen, you arrogant arse-wipe." Igneus' voice cracked across the tavern like a whip, sharp enough to cut through the rising din of drunken chatter. He stepped forward, muscled frame filling the gap between Valcom and the slouched, belligerent patron. With deliberate force, he slammed a freshly filled mug onto the bar so hard that froth spilled over the rim and ran down the wood. "Down this drink and then get out of my brother's business. You don't like how he runs things? Go drink piss water in a different pub."

The man glared, half rising from his stool as though considering a fight, but something in Igneus' steel-eyed stare made him think better of it. With a grumble that was more like a growl, he snatched the mug, swallowed hard, and slunk away into the crowd, muttering curses under his breath.

Igneus didn't watch him go. He turned back to Valcom, who stood behind the bar collecting the empty mug with silence and sorrow. His eyes, dark and heavy-lidded, seemed far older than the face they were set in.

"We're at the edge of the village," Igneus muttered, lowering his voice as he wiped foam from his knuckles. "We get all the town's windsuckers here. That's all he is—jealous."

Valcom didn't answer. He rinsed the basin, water sloshing softly. Then, as if dragging words up from a place he didn't want to visit, he asked, "Do you think… Have you ever wondered why I became a tavern keeper?"

Igneus raised a brow, surprised by the question. A woman, cheeks flushed with ale, drifted toward Valcom, but Igneus cut her off with a wave of his arm, herded her back toward the hearth. He leaned against the shelf of bottles, arms crossed, a wall of casual strength. "Not really," he admitted. "Why?"

Valcom picked up a rag, his fingers ginger on the glass of the mug as though it might shatter with too much force. His voice was low. "Well, because of—"

"Ohh." Understanding struck Igneus, blunt and ugly. His face tightened. "That bastard's dead, Valcom. We don't have to care about him anymore."

Valcom's shoulders sagged. He let out a long sigh, the kind that rattled in the chest. "We've been bastards ever since we were born."

The silence that followed was thick, heavy as smoke.

"Including Miriana," Igneus whispered finally. "Ever since they left. Is that right?"

Valcom turned, rag dripping, hand clenched so tight around it that water streamed between his fingers. His jaw trembled, though his eyes stayed steady. "I'm tired of giving everyone the benefit of the doubt. They've already proven who they are. I've finally realized…" His voice cracked with restrained fury. "I have more bullshit to deal with than everyone else's."

He turned back to the bar, forcing his breath slow, forcing his hands steady as he wiped down the counter and greeted the huffy woman who had returned, demanding her drink with a tap of her nails.

"Good," Igneus muttered, his voice a low rumble as he moved behind the bar toward the door. He nodded at his brother. "Finally."

Later, when the tavern's rush had thinned and the night grew deep, Igneus sat alone at the bar. He poured himself a brew from the pitcher. He drank and ignored the laughter and the occasional argument sparking in the corners. The world blurred at the edges as he slipped further into himself.

Another drink. Then another. Until he was somewhere else entirely.

***

A young Igneus walked down the dirt road, boots too big for his feet, kicking a pebble that danced ahead of him. It clattered against other stones, skittered into dust, rolled into a rut. The air smelled of dry hay and damp wood, the sun falling low and fat on the horizon.

He passed a broken-down mill. Its boards were warped and covered in a greenish-black crust of moss or mold; no one could tell the difference. The place stank with a pungent rot that clung to the throat.

"Stop!" a voice shouted from inside.

Igneus froze. The sound of wailing followed, high and ragged, tangled with shouts. His feet felt nailed to the ground.

The door slammed open and a man stumbled out. His chest heaved, sweat streaking his dirt-stained face. He wiped his hand on his trousers, which left a red streak behind. His brown tunic was torn wide across the middle, revealing angry scratches beneath. Igneus' gaze dropped and caught on the dagger tucked neatly into the man's boot.

The stranger's eyes flicked to him. He assessed Igneus sharply and then gave him a curt nod, as if the boy had passed some test by simply standing there.

"Stop!" Another figure burst through the doorway. He was a rounder man, face blotched crimson, a heavy mallet raised above his head. His voice cracked with desperation, high and almost pleading, even as he hurled curses.

The first man grabbed Igneus' arm. His grip was iron, unyielding. "Time to go," he barked, dragging him down the road.

"Wait—!" Igneus twisted, his heels scraped against the dirt, but the man hauled him forward, faster and faster, until the mill and the shouting man fell away behind them. They didn't stop until the trees thinned and the crash of waves reached their ears, the village left far behind.

Igneus yanked his arm free, chest burning. "Who are you? What did you do?"

The man turned, wiping his brow. His smile was thin, feral. "I'm going to collect my pay."

"What?"

"Boy," he huffed, adjusting his tunic, "I killed a bad man. I was charged with killing a bad man. I have to meet my client."

Igneus blinked, heart hammering. "So… you're a good guy?"

The man's smile widened just slightly, though it didn't quite reach his eyes. He turned to go. "Yeah. It's a living, kid."

"Igneus," the boy blurted, needing to anchor himself with something real.

The man glanced back once, the sea wind tugging at his torn tunic. "Romof."

After that night, Igneus often sought the man out. Romof was a shadow on the edges of the village, drifting in and out of places children were told never to go. To Igneus, he was more than a shadow. He was everything his young heart longed for: bravery, defiance, freedom.

Romof taught him to fight. At first, it was clumsy sparring with sticks. Igneus stumbled and got bruised, but grinned widely. Then came real blades, real strikes. Every scar was a lesson. Every lesson, a secret treasure.

One day, when Igneus had grown taller, stronger, Romof beckoned him with a tilt of his head. "Walk with me," he said. And Igneus followed, never once looking back.

CHAPTER FOUR

"*Do you really wish to join our alliance? It is not such a lighthearted group,*" *Romof questioned in a low and commanding voice. He stood at the center of the clearing, the clear leader among the gathered men. His saber's gold hilt gleamed in the torchlight, polished though marred with abrasions that caught the glow like scattered diamonds. The weapon was as much a symbol as it was a threat.*

Igneus was kneeling on the forest floor, damp earth pressing against his knees. Around him, torches flared with their flames bending and twisting in the restless night breeze. Shadows leapt and writhed across the trees, making the whole gathering seem alive with unseen specters. Encircling him were several broad-shouldered men, their frames filling out the dark red tunics they wore. The tunics dipped low at the neckline to flaunt the branded mark carved into their flesh: a ring with a wing breaking from its circle, splattered as though dipped in blood. The burn looked raw even on their hardened skin, a badge of belonging that carried equal parts pride and menace.

Igneus grimaced, his eyes flicking over the symbol.

"*I created this band because I wanted to mean something. There is an evil in this world, Igneus. With us clearing away the cockroaches and making the way safe.*"

Romof gestured toward the center of the clearing, where the earth had been worn bare. He led Igneus into that space, and the rest of the men stepped back, arranging themselves into a wider circle. Their cloaks shifted like blood-dark banners in the torchlight.

"Do you want to be a part of a movement?" Romof asked with a strange reverence as they entered the circle's heart.

"I have nowhere else to go," Igneus sighed. His voice was heavy and weighted with resignation. Meeting Romof's eyes without flinching, he tugged the neckline of his cream tunic down and bared his shoulder.

Romof's slow smile spread, sharp and certain. *"Bring it."* He snapped his fingers.

One of the men stepped forward from Romof's right. He was expressionless, his features carved into a mask of duty. From a shrub at the circle's edge, he drew out a brand stick half-hidden among the branches. He pressed its iron tip into a nearby torch until it glowed, a small sun of molten orange.

When he returned to Igneus, the brand in his grip hissed faintly, smoke rising from its edge. Without hesitation, he yanked Igneus' tunic further down and thrust the heated iron into his shoulder blade.

The scream that tore from Igneus' throat echoed through the forest, startling birds into flight. The sharp scent of charred flesh filled the clearing, acrid and thick, burning its way into every nostril. The sizzling noise seemed to stretch time itself, each second an eternity of pain. Igneus' body shook, but through a grimace he forced himself to remain upright, fighting the urge to collapse.

When the iron was finally lifted away, a patch of blistered, blackened skin smoked in the torchlight. One of the men's gazes lingered on a nearby flame, mesmerized by how it resembled a tongue licking hungrily at the night, bending towards Igneus.

Igneus adjusted his tunic back into place with a trembling hand, breathing hard. The man with the brand retreated, his bleak face as unreadable as stone.

Romof stepped forward, his smile dazzling, warm as the sun yet dangerous in its brilliance. "Welcome to the gang, Igneus. Glad to have you with us."

Igneus, still shaking, managed a tight smile despite the searing pain. "Good to be with ya."

As one, the men in red tunics stepped back in perfect synchronization. The movement was crisp, rehearsed, almost ritualistic. Igneus frowned at the gesture, but Romof dismissed his suspicion with a casual wave, beckoning him to follow. Together, they left the ring of torches, the other men falling in line behind like shadows stretching into the forest.

"Do you know why I started this little band, friend?" Romof asked as they walked. His tone softened into something melodic, almost hypnotic, his words sliding like a siren's song through the dark.

"Give the bad community their dues," Igneus said simply.

Romof tipped his head back and laughed, rough and hoarse, the sound rolling through the trees like a barked challenge.

"I like you, kid. Have I said that?"

Igneus shook his head silently.

"Well, I am now. And yes, to give them their dues, as you innocently put it. You've got the makings of a tough man, Igneus. But thinking of our foes as only the 'bad community' is far too simple. Life ain't like that." Romof's gaze flicked to him from the corner of his eye, studying.

They stopped, and Romof laid a heavy hand on Igneus' shoulder. His grip was firm, his expression unreadable.

"Why are you doing this, son?"

The word struck Igneus like a blade. He bristled, his body shifting away instinctively. His silence spoke volumes.

"Ah," Romof murmured knowingly. "Personal, huh?"

Igneus met his eyes with a small, sheepish smile. There was something so young, so trusting about him, as if he hadn't yet learned the cost of trust.

"I needed to get out of a rough spot. Nowhere to go. Trapped," Romof said softly, continuing forward. His tone was confessional, his steps deliberate. Igneus followed, warmth blooming in his chest, mistaking Romof's words for kinship.

What a fool he had been. So trusting. So naïve.

"You don't have to explain it to me, of course," Romof went on, clapping Igneus' shoulder once more. "But if you ever wanted to, or needed to—I'm here."

He gave a final pat, then strode ahead into the forest shadows, leaving Igneus in the clearing's edge.

"Oh," he called back over his shoulder, "and allow people to see the brand. It helps promote yourself, your job, without making it too obvious." He winked, then disappeared between the trees.

Igneus lifted his fingers to the raw, stinging brand. Despite the pain, a smile tugged at his lips.

Stupid, stupid, stupid. If only he could go back and change that.

Igneus hunched at the bar, downing another mug of ale with a practiced tilt of the wrist. He reached for the pitcher with one hand while wiping foam from his mouth with the other. The warmth of the brew spread through him in waves. First his chest, then his arms, then curling into his fingertips and toes. His fist closed clumsily around the pitcher's cold metal handle, the chill cutting through his fleeting comfort. He poured, watching the bark-colored liquid rise into his mug, the froth swelling like a pale cloud drifting across a storm-dark sky. For a moment, even the sight of it lifted his spirits.

"How much have you had?" Valcom's voice cut in, steady and unimpressed. He came up to the bar after clearing a table, balancing a stack of dirty bowls and mugs. The tavern buzzed behind him, full of clattering dishes and bursts of laughter. Smoke from the fire pit hung in the rafters like a low haze, mingling with the tang of spilled ale and stewed onions. Patrons barked orders for bread or stew, meals Valcom had cooked the night before and reheated for the evening rush.

He dropped the filthy dishes into a wooden basin by the bar, water splashing as he poured in a fresh bucket and tossed in a rag.

"Not enough," Igneus muttered, raising the mug to his lips. The heat returned with the swallow, mellowing his expression.

Valcom didn't answer immediately. Instead, he reached over, yanked the pitcher from Igneus' hand, and without ceremony dumped its contents onto the floor. The ale hissed as it splattered across the wood planks, soaking into cracks already darkened with years of spilled drink. He tossed the empty vessel into the basin with a clatter, letting it join the pile of greasy plates and mugs.

"Hey!" Igneus protested.

"You still have that mug," Valcom pointed out. His tone was clipped but even, as though lecturing a child. "The last one you'll have tonight."

He wrung out the rag and began scrubbing, his movements brisk, sharp with frustration.

"I was starting to feel better," Igneus moaned, staring mournfully at the pale foam still clinging to his mug's rim. He brought it to his nose, inhaling the remnants like perfume.

"That would only last for a little while, brother. Wait till tomorrow," Valcom jabbed, not looking up.

Igneus squinted at him blearily. "Wait till tomorrow for more ale, or wait till tomorrow to feel the ale I had today?" He tipped the mug higher, shaking it, tapping the bottom with his palm to coax out every lingering drop. His throat worked greedily as he swallowed.

"You're pathetic," Valcom sighed. He plucked the mug from Igneus' hand and tossed it into the basin with the others. The pile rattled with the sound of clinking glass and ceramic.

Several more patrons shuffled forward, coins clinking in their palms. Valcom moved seamlessly from scolding his brother to serving customers, taking the mugs and pitchers he had just cleaned, filling them from the fresh keg, and sliding them across the bar with swift precision. Copper and silver clinked into his palm, and he slipped the coins into a wooden box without missing a beat.

Only then did he turn back to Igneus, who was staring forlornly at his now-empty hand as if it had betrayed him.

"Both," Valcom said flatly.

"Huh?" Igneus blinked up at him drunkenly, words heavy on his tongue.

"You're going to be miserable tomorrow. And you can have more tomorrow. Only if you pay for it."

Igneus scoffed, slumping against the bar. "But we're brothers. I don't have to pay."

That made Valcom pause. He froze with the rag still in hand and slowly turned. His eyes narrowed, tired but sharp.

"We are brothers," he said evenly, "but I'm trying to run an establishment here."

Igneus glanced around with exaggerated confusion, muttering something about what kind of establishment this even was. The crowd was rowdy, the tables scarred, the air thick with sweat and smoke, yet beneath all that grime, there was a sense of belonging.

Valcom gave a dramatic gasp, his patience cracking, and tried to shoo his brother away from the bar. Igneus shook his head and muttered something about going on a walk before leaving.

At the far end of the bar, Miriana had been watching over the edge of her book. She smiled faintly at their bickering before piping up, her voice cutting through the tavern's din.

"Valcom, you never talk about why you became a barkeep. Why?"

Valcom's smile faltered. His hands stilled on the rag. For a long moment, the only sound was the tavern's hum around them: dice clattering on tabletops, boots stamping to a fiddler's tune, the crack of laughter splitting the smoke-laden air.

Finally, he spoke. His voice was low, steady, carrying the weight of memory.

"I was considered a runt. I was born late and tiny. The youngest. My father thought 'tough love' was the only type of love." He shook his head. "All children had to do chores, true. But no five-year-old should work manual labor. I would get blisters, slivers, and come crying to my mother for help."

His face hardened, jaw clenched. "My father would look down on me. Spit at me. Hit me. He would say, 'A real man takes his burdens to push up the hill. If he slips'," Valcom gave a bitter laugh, "'then he is no man.'"

His voice grew softer. "Your father, the eldest, tried to help. He thought kindness could fix it. Told me things like, 'He doesn't mean it,' or, 'I think you're enough.' But to my father, that only made it worse. To him, it meant I was pathetic for believing such lies. Simon was the strong one, the noble one, while I was nothing."

Valcom's eyes fell to the wood grain of the bar, tracing the cracks. His words thinned to a whisper. "My mother had been broken long before. That marriage began with love, but it rotted. He chose his favorites, and she decided it was fruitless to get in the way."

He gestured faintly around the room, his rag limp in his hand. "He didn't much care for Igneus, didn't even notice him half the time. But me… he hated me. This—" he swept his arm to take in the tavern's smoky rafters, the crowded tables, the laughter ringing off its walls— "this was their house. I wanted it to be something good. A place where people could gather and speak. Meet, eat, belong."

He fell quiet. For a heartbeat, even the tavern's roar seemed to fade.

"I sometimes wonder," Valcom admitted, his voice rough, "if I became somewhat like the people who caused me my worries."

He let the rag drop back into the basin, the splash ringing louder than it should.

He poured himself a fresh brew and chugged it all in one long swallow, the amber liquid spilling down his chin and trailing along his Adam's apple. He refilled the mug without hesitation, the motion practiced, almost mechanical.

Miriana, sitting nearby, watched in silence. Her eyes dimmed at the sight of him locked in this sad cycle—drink, swallow, refill, repeat. With a sigh, she placed her open book down on the table, its spine balanced delicately against the wood, and rose to her feet. Slowly, gently, she wrapped her arms around his midsection.

Valcom gave a startled jolt, nearly choking on the mouthful of ale. He sputtered, setting the mug down with a dull thud before awkwardly placing his arms across her back.

"I love you," she whispered into his chest.

A tear slipped down Valcom's cheek and disappeared into her dark hair. "Thank you," he murmured, his voice hoarse. He pulled back enough to look at her, forcing a small, fleeting smile.

"I wish my brother and I could give you a nobler life."

"Well, I like this one just fine," she replied with a smile of her own, the kind that was both stubborn and reassuring. She slipped back to her seat at the bar, picking up her book to the folded page. The candlelight caught the faint smudge of her birthmark as she brushed a braid back behind her ear.

Valcom watched her, his smile faint but tinged with something wistful. "Do you know what Igneus used to call you when you were a baby?"

Miriana sighed, her eyes still skimming the page. "Your hero," she said softly, rubbing her birthmark with one hand, almost self-conscious.

The tavern door squeaked just then, hinges groaning as it shut behind the figure stepping inside. The draft of cool night air curled through the smoky room.

"I should go back to calling you that. Our hero!" Igneus' voice rang out, full of cheer. He stomped the dirt from his boots, the sound like gravel scattering across the floorboards, and strode toward the counter. With a grin, he reached out to rub his niece's head. Her braid snapped like a whip across her shoulder as she swatted his hand away, though a reluctant smile tugged at her lips.

"Because you are strong in our struggles," Valcom added, turning his gaze on his brother. "And where have you been? I thought you promised me you were going to help with the dinner rush? You're lucky it's slowing down now." His raised brow carried the weight of long disappointment.

"I was planning," Igneus huffed, dropping heavily onto a stool as if the weight of his excuses alone held him down.

Valcom and Miriana exchanged a look—half weary, half amused. They both smiled, though the edges of those smiles felt thin, strained.

Valcom plunged a pitcher into a barrel of crisp beer, the froth sloshing up the sides. Setting the filled vessel down on the counter, he looked squarely into his brother's eyes. "Why bother showing up now if you missed the promise altogether?"

Igneus scoffed. "I wasn't aware promises had deadlines."

"Interesting," Valcom snided, his tone sharp as a knife. "One would assume you'd know all about deadlines in the kind of occupation you're in."

Miriana shut her book with a snap, marking her page with her thumb. "If you two are just going to argue," she said, "I'm leaving."

"No, don't go," Igneus interjected quickly. He spread his arms as if to draw her back into the circle of their quarrel. "Settle this for us, our hero. Both your uncles have jobs they hate—"

"Speak for yourself," Valcom cut in without missing a beat.

"Oh, so you do like working in this hellhole?" Igneus spat back.

Miriana rolled her eyes and, shaking her head, slowly shuffled out of the tavern. The door creaked again as it shut behind her, leaving the two brothers facing each other across the counter.

"You always did cause trouble," Valcom snapped, voice low but sharp.

"Please," Igneus countered with a sneer. "You're just sour because you went from doing all the chores to doing whatever it is you want."

"Leave!" Valcom's voice rose, anger flashing. He slammed the mug he had been cleaning onto the bar, the wood groaning beneath the impact. "You keep complaining and fighting against it. You've killed many people, Igneus! And now you suddenly grow a conscience when it comes to the royal family?"

"I don't know what will happen to the island! The people!" Igneus shot back, his voice trembling between guilt and defiance.

"That didn't stop you before!" Valcom's eyes blazed. "What were you thinking, joining 'The Wings of Massacre'?"

Igneus' jaw clenched, but his words came raw and fast. "I was thinking I wanted to do my own things! Find my own path. But I was young and foolish. I wanted to be a part of something. I never had my own thing."

Valcom ladled broth into bowls with harsh, deliberate motions, his frustration echoing in every movement. He shoved the bowls onto trays and began weaving between tables to deliver them.

"You could have worked with me," he said over his shoulder. "You still can. Just go into hiding. Fake your death, even. Maybe that would save you."

"Fake my death," Igneus scoffed, shaking his head. "They'd never believe it. Anyway…" He trailed off, his voice dropping lower, his bravado softening. A flush crept into his cheeks. "I don't enjoy… what I do."

For once, his words hung heavy in the smoky tavern air, unchallenged.

Valcom looked at him, his expression softening though his eyes remained stern. "Of course you wouldn't. You got this job because you left the cottage to make your own, except there is a fee at every checkpoint on every path, my blood." He stepped closer, his boots creaking against the tavern's old floorboards, and placed a comforting hand on Igneus' shoulder. His grip was firm, steady. "These are lives you are taking. Flawed, yes. But so are you. You cannot be the one to decide who goes. That destroys a man. I don't want to see you destroyed."

At that moment, the tavern's door creaked open again. A chill wind slithered inside, carrying the scent of damp earth. A figure cloaked in green drifted into the establishment, the hood drawn so low their face was swallowed in shadow. The noise of laughter, clinking mugs, and shouts for stew from the tavern carried on around them, but at the doorway, everything was still.

Raising an arm hidden deep within the folds of the sleeve, the figure gestured to Igneus and then toward the window. The motion was deliberate, commanding.

Igneus looked at his brother, who only shook his head slowly, disappointment etched across his face.

"Valcom—" Igneus began.

"Your client needs you," Valcom cut him off curtly, his tone cold.

Igneus looked at his boots and followed the ghost outside. It whirled on him when the door shut behind them both.

A voice hissed from under the hood, sharp and serpentine. "You haven't done the deed!"

Igneus arched a brow, leaning slightly to peer into the depths of the cowl. All he saw was shadow. His gaze flicked around the tavern—it was still loud, still bustling, as though no one else even noticed the presence of this spirit-like intruder.

"I can't," Igneus said firmly, turning away. "It'll cast all of Sorcerac into chaos. I will be hunted. I have enemies already, but the castle's people will forever bother my family. I can't have that." He began walking toward the forest, pushing through the door into the night air. "There will be no leader, and the power will be up for grabs. it will cause an all-out civil war."

The cloaked figure's voice sharpened with indignation, shrill and cutting. "Look who has gained a conscience all of a sudden. So, the king and queen's lives matter more than all the other lives you have slain?"

Igneus turned slowly, the torchlight outside catching on the hard lines of his face. He didn't move closer, but his posture stiffened.

"Those were evil people," he said, his voice deliberate. "They killed and hurt others. The king and queen are innocent. They have ruled for years. To upset the balance like that is madness."

A high-pitched laugh split the night, wild and scornful. "Innocent?! Innocent?! They are human beings. There is no innocence. You are common folk! You have no idea what they are like. No idea!"

Igneus crossed his arms, his jaw tight. "If you want someone to do something for you, I wouldn't insult them or their 'folk.'"

The two stood in tense silence, the cloaked figure glaring from the shadows of their hood, the air between them thick with challenge.

"In what way, other than being human, have they committed guilt?" Igneus pressed, taking a few slow steps forward, closing the distance with measured defiance.

The cloaked figure shifted, their sigh dripping with indignation. "You know nothing of politics," they spat.

Igneus shook his head. "As much as I would love a change in the kingdom, there would be unbridled chaos. Corpses everywhere. An all-out war."

The figure's cape rustled violently, as if caught by a phantom wind. From the folds of their cloak, they produced a chrome saber that gleamed under the torchlight. Its edge jagged like a dragon's tooth. They pointed it directly at Igneus' chest.

Igneus' hand slid toward the knives strapped at his belt.

"I wouldn't," the figure warned, their voice deadly calm. "I've been told I'm a quick carver. Or at least, they would say, if they were still living."

Reluctantly, Igneus lifted his hands above his head, each motion slow and begrudging. His glare never left the hooded figure.

"How come I need to murder the king and queen, if you are such a 'quick carver'?" he demanded.

The figure circled him like a predator, the saber unwavering at his torso until they were certain he would not strike. Then, with practiced grace, they slid the weapon back into its sheath. It was only then that Igneus noticed the spotless white gloves covering their hands, untouched by dirt, blood, or labor.

"Let's just say I am in too deep to do it myself," the figure said with a hiss. "Ergo, you are being paid to do this chore."

Igneus snorted, folding his arms across his chest again. "I don't know how well I feel about being paid for a 'chore', especially by someone who thinks killing royalty is a chore." He began to pace slowly, circling the figure in return. "You say you're in too deep. What does that mean? Who are you?"

The figure's voice turned cold as steel. "I'm done with these questions." They reached into their cloak, the faint gleam of gold flashing in the dark. "Hopefully no one ends you—or others, now that you know what is wanted."

"One person against three?" Igneus tilted his head, a dangerous grin flickering. "Those are pretty good odds."

Quicker than a blink, the stranger pressed a dagger up beneath his throat. The blade's chill kissed his skin, and his pulse hammered against it.

"Don't cross me, bumpkin," the figure growled, their voice guttural and low now, stripped of its shrillness. "I have friends in high places. Even if your family somehow defeated me, they would be dead within a week. Everyone affiliated with you? Gone."

The dagger lingered at his neck a moment longer, just enough to bite. Then the figure withdrew it, vanishing the blade back into the folds of the cloak as though it had never existed. Without another word, they turned and marched into the darkness, their green cloak trailing like a shadow given flesh.

Igneus let out a long breath he hadn't realized he was holding. His shoulders sagged as the tension left him. Slowly, he turned back toward the tavern.

Inside, the noise of raucous laughter, stamping boots, and the crackle of fire filled the air. Life carried on as if nothing had happened.

Igneus slipped through the back, his steps heavy, and retreated to his small apartment. The room was sparse: three cots, with his tucked beneath the only window, a rickety table listing to one side. The silence pressed in thick and suffocating, and for the first time in a long while, Igneus felt alone.

He crouched down, pushing aside a few loose floorboards and searching under his cot for his ragged cloak. The room was dim, the faint moonlight slipping through the window doing little to soften the shadows clinging to the corners. The rickety cot creaked as he lifted it slightly, dust motes drifting lazily in the pale light.

The door creaked open behind him.

"They won't accept it, you know," came his brother's voice, worn thin from a long day of pouring dizzying concoctions and sparring words. The tone was tired, almost flat.

Igneus turned sharply, his hand still tangled in the fabric beneath the bed. His eyes widened. Valcom stood in the doorway, but his figure was pale, almost spectral. The blond hair that usually caught the glow of the tavern lamps was dulled to a sickly grey in the moonlight. His face carried a froggy green hue, and his eyes seemed hollow, as though the weight of exhaustion had carved purple shadows deep beneath them. His frame appeared thinner and frailer, though Igneus prayed it was only his imagination or some cruel trick of the light.

"Your 'leaving,' I mean," Valcom clarified, his voice still steady despite his ghostly appearance. "They'll take it as an act of war, retaliate, and pillage the coinage—and carry out the task anyway."

Igneus didn't answer. He only stared, caught between confusion and dread, before tearing his gaze away and returning to his search under the cot. The silence stretched thin between them.

"Igneus," Valcom said again, softer this time. "It won't end well." He paused, reading the look his brother had given him. Then, as though to lighten the mood, he added with a half-smile, "I'm fine. This is the body of a hard worker." A dry chuckle escaped him, though it carried little warmth.

Igneus pressed his lips together and kept rummaging, unwilling to engage further.

"It will have the same outcome if you don't go through with it," Valcom continued, shifting against the molding doorframe. He rubbed his back against the wood as though trying to work out a stubborn kink. "The danger is always the same."

"Valcom, please," Igneus begged suddenly, whirling to face him. His voice cracked under the weight of his words. In his hands now was a maroon cloak, the fabric faded but sturdy.

"I'm surrounded by criminals," Valcom burst out, the frustration boiling over at last. His voice echoed off the small room's walls, sharp and ragged. "You. Then Miriana and her friends grew up far too quickly. They are thieving to provide for their families. They are kids. We should be doing better."

"This is the last job," Igneus hissed back, his tone laced with desperation. He threw the cloak around his shoulders, the maroon folds falling across him like a shroud. His hands shook slightly as he fastened it at his throat. "Where is she, anyway?"

Valcom exhaled heavily, his jaw tight. He turned away without another word, his hand brushing the doorframe as he stepped into the hall. "She's in town," he said at last, his voice low, before disappearing into the shadows beyond the doorway.

CHAPTER FIVE

In the town square, a lute's melody floated through the warm air, weaving between the chatter and footsteps like a silken thread. Its notes carried a mischievous charm, tugging at ears and hearts alike, pulling onlookers into its orbit. Then came the voice, sweet, clear, and laced with a haunting beauty, the one that lured them even closer.

A small crowd gathered around the twins. Neel strummed his lute with playful flourish, spinning in wide circles around the prettiest young women. He winked shamelessly, earning scoffs and flushed cheeks in equal measure. At the circle's heart, Amalia swayed with the trees that fringed the square, her soprano voice so poignant that birds wheeled above her as though answering her call.

Few noticed the figure darting between them, cloaked in navy and moving with quiet precision. Miriana slipped through the bodies like a shadow among weeds. Her deft hands dipped into purses, lifting coins only to replace them with smooth pebbles, keeping the weight unchanged. Rings slid from fingers, necklaces vanished from throats. All while the music and singing masked the soft rustle of her movements.

Her hands rested casually in her cloak's pockets, stifling the jangle of stolen trinkets that seemed to giggle at their escape. Ahead of her stood a large man in a rough brown smock tied with nothing but rope. His head was bald on top, with only a dusting of grey hair clinging stubbornly at the sides.

The old friar, Miriana mused, eyeing him with mischief. She lingered, feigning admiration of the music while her gaze fixed on the golden ring gleaming mockingly from his finger, winking at her in the sunlight. Prosperous work, indeed. Information worth remembering.

"Friar!" she exclaimed brightly. "How kind of you to listen to the young folk play the Lord's heartbeat. Such a kind and high friar."

The friar turned, a blush of pink rising to his cheeks. He smiled indulgently. "Daughter, there is only one higher than me, but I thank you for such magnificent words. You make me feel so joyous."

Neel struck up a livelier tune, and both twins hooted and hollered as they twirled, their laughter infectious. The crowd's delight swelled, people clapping and dancing along in a tide of merriment.

The friar grew restless, his attention tugged toward the spectacle. Miriana seized her moment. She grasped his hand, bowed low, and pressed her lips lightly to his knuckles. With a smooth twist, she slid the ring from his finger. Another bow, a flourish, and she melted back into the crowd, leaving the holy man staring after her, none the wiser. Until he cups his hands together on his rotund body.

"Thief!" the friar shrieked, his voice shrill as he jabbed his bare finger toward Miriana's retreating figure.

Heads turned. The crowd surged in on her, suspicion and fury rippling through them.

Then—crack! The splintering sound of wood tore the tension. Neel stood panting, his lute shattered at his feet, shards glittering like teeth around him and Amalia. The crowd's focus wavered, scattering just enough for Miriana to stagger away through the gap.

"Stop, thief!" voices cried.

"She's getting away!"

"Thank you all, you've been a lovely audience!" Amalia shouted, grabbing Neel's hand as the twins bolted after their friend. The crowd followed, the square dissolving into chaos.

"Where are we going?" Amalia hollered as her boots pounded against the cobblestones.

"The hell if I know!" Miriana wheezed, darting around a corner. Together they shoved crates into the street, slowing their pursuers. A thought flared in Miriana's mind.

"Head to the tree!" she shouted back.

"What?!" Neel bellowed. "What the hell does that mean?!"

But Miriana was already veering sharply right at the alley's end.

"Stop! You are wanted men!" guards bellowed, surging forward with armored arms outstretched.

Miriana shoved open a doorway to a building. They ran through avoiding all the inhabitants with Miriana leading her friends through. They burst into open air again, now on the high tower walkways. Boots thundered across the stone bridge connecting the towers.

"Stop, criminals!" The guards' voices grew louder. Their pursuit closed in, the distance shrinking with each breath. Amalia, lagging behind, felt a gauntleted hand swipe the air just shy of her shoulder. She squealed, lungs burning.

"Does yelling at us to stop ever work?" Neel shouted between breaths. "Why would we stop?!"

Both Miriana and Amalia shot him sharp glares, their eyes promising retribution later. His cheeks burned pink, but he kept running.

They burst into a neighboring tower, finding themselves in a turret chamber with nowhere to go but back. A massive cannon loomed in the center like a sleeping beast. Behind them, the guards poured into the tower, their armored march echoing up the stone walls.

A blue haze filled the edges of Miriana's vision. She pressed a hand to her forehead, trying to block the glare of the sun, but the strange light persisted.

"You are to come with us," one guard thundered, voice booming in the chamber.

The three friends took a panicked step back, their heels scraping against the stones. Miriana glanced behind her. The red triangular flag above the tower whipped furiously in the wind.

Her voice dropped to a whisper. "Do you trust me?"

"Yes," Amalia whimpered, her body trembling as the guards advanced.

"Why? Why are you asking us now?" Neel barked, confusion plain in his voice.

Miriana didn't answer. She was already climbing onto the wall, her boots scraping against the stone. Both twins froze, wide-eyed.

"Follow me. Now. If you want out of this," she hissed through clenched teeth.

Neel exchanged a look with Amalia. Without further hesitation, they scrambled after her, hearts hammering.

"What are you—" a guard began, striding forward.

Miriana cut him off by seizing both siblings, yanking their arms around her shoulders. "Hold on."

"They're going to jump!" a soldier bellowed, his voice cracking with disbelief.

"What?" Amalia gasped, her stomach twisting. She stared at Miriana as though she'd gone mad.

But there was no time to protest. With a sudden, fierce movement, Miriana flung herself backward into open air, dragging Neel and Amalia with her.

The world flipped. The three of them screamed, their voices lost in the roar of the wind rushing past. Neel's grip tightened until his knuckles whitened. Amalia buried her face in Miriana's shoulder.

At the last instant, Miriana reached out and caught hold of the flag whipping from the tower. The fabric stretched, groaned, then began to rip beneath their combined weight. It slowed them, but barely. The flag tore with a loud crack, and they plummeted, hitting the cobblestone with bone-jarring force.

They rolled in a tangled heap. Amalia groaned and rolled away, clutching her side. Neel released Miriana at once, sitting up with a pale, furious face.

"Never do that again," he panted, his voice shaking more than he wanted to admit.

Above them, soldiers crowded the battlements, shouting and pointing. A few already began their descent.

"Split up!" Miriana shouted. She bolted down the nearest alley without checking if her friends followed.

Later, the town was far behind her. Miriana leaned against the familiar willow, nestled in the crook of its sturdy arms above the ground. A book lay open in her lap, its pages ruffled by the breeze. As a child, she had run here to escape the cruel children who mocked her. Here, in this glen, her uncles had raised her.

Valcom had taught her to read and write, often saying, "Think of the power that can come from a cunning mind." Igneus had taught her to fight, turning their games into lessons of survival. She remembered sparring with brittle branches, their shouts echoing as they ducked, lunged, and parried against invisible foes. This tree had been her fortress, her classroom, her home.

She turned the page just as a rustle came from the undergrowth. The sound was sharp enough to make her tense. Gently, she set the book aside, creasing the corner to mark her place. In one fluid motion she unsheathed her sword and leapt down, landing with a solid thud.

"Who's there?!" she demanded, her voice ringing.

Two familiar shapes stumbled from the brush, hands raised. Neel and Amalia, flushed and panting, blinking as though caught in torchlight.

"You always get so touchy whenever you're around this tree," Neel teased breathlessly.

Miriana let out a half-snort. "Well, yeah. It's where I feel safest."

She studied them a moment, the tension easing from her shoulders. Their hair was wild, their clothes torn and smeared with dust. Bruises and scratches dotted their skin, badges of the chase they'd barely escaped.

"Finally shook off the suckers, did you?" she asked, pulling them both into a tight embrace. "Took you long enough. I read about five chapters waiting for you."

Amalia laughed as they pulled apart. "One, you read too fast. Two, you run too fast. Three, you disappeared."

Miriana smirked and began climbing back into the willow, her boots finding the familiar knobs in the bark. "One, you said I ran fast. Two, that's what splitting up is."

The three settled among the branches, as they had so many times before, letting the sway of the tree soothe their racing hearts.

"Where's the loot?" Neel asked at last, grinning.

Miriana reached higher into the branches, retrieving a black sack. She dropped it onto the broad arm of the tree with a soft thump. Together they sifted through the treasures, ensuring each had an even share of trinkets and coins.

"If we're going to keep doing this to make a living," Amalia said after a while, her voice thoughtful, "we'll need a hiding place. Somewhere safe."

Miriana looked around the glen. The dense wall of trees created a natural fortress. The willow's broad arms embraced them, just as it always had. Here, her uncles had made sure she had a childhood. Here, she had always felt untouchable.

"Why don't we build a home here?" she breathed, almost in awe of the idea.

"I'm sorry, what?" Neel was too busy using the gleam of a stolen chalice to examine his teeth.

"Why don't we build a sanctuary?" she said more firmly. "A hideout in the tree. Far from people. Secluded. Ours."

They both looked up at her, studying her face, weighing the likelihood that this was a jest. But no— this was Miriana at her most Miriana, fierce and unflinching, her truest self perched upon the boughs of her childhood sanctuary. She would not cast aside such a vision lightly, not even for thievery's fleeting spoils.

"Miriana…" Amalia began cautiously.

"Well, why not?" Miriana's voice sharpened, her conviction already kindling. She stood and began pacing the broad branch, her boots leaving shallow grooves in the bark. "My family's been through hell and back. You both know this. And what do we do now? You play music for audiences of one or two—"

"It's been three before," Neel muttered, defensive.

Miriana ignored him, her steps quickening with her thoughts. "Why can't there be more for us? More for all of us? Let's make more. Let's do it!"

Amalia turned a bracelet over in her hands, the golden links catching the fading light. Her brow furrowed. "Um… do what?" she asked, tilting her head like a pup trying to catch the sense of someone's words.

"Be heroes!" Miriana cried. She dropped suddenly to a seated position, swinging her legs out and landing with a bounce on another arm of the tree. Her eyes shone. "Of course we'll need funds, so we'll steal a while longer. But then, we'll repay it by saving people. By changing things."

Her gaze drifted skyward, and her voice softened to a murmur. "Maybe the world."

Neel and Amalia stared at her, then at each other, incredulous.

"The world?" Amalia scoffed gently. "What exactly do you think we'll be doing?"

"Yeah," Neel chimed in. "We're thieves and bards. What's the world ever done for us?"

Miriana's eyes snapped back to them. She looked around at the willow, at the sanctuary her uncles had given her, at the stolen trinkets glimmering like false stars in the twilight. Then she fixed her gaze on her friends, her voice suddenly plain and steady.

"Exactly," she said. "The world has given us nothing. So we'll give to ourselves. We'll put in the work, and we'll reap the rewards."

Neel and Amalia stopped fingering their treasures. Her words hung in the air, heavy and strange.

Miriana could see saving those around her, the crowds chanting her name, praise raining down like sunlight. Never again would her family or friends go hungry. Never again would the world turn its back on them.

"Everyone loves a hero," she whispered. An idea sparked in her mind, catching like kindling. Soon it blazed, wild and unstoppable.

Now all we have to do is find trouble, she thought.

The very next day, trouble found them.

The castle gates loomed, and before the friends could blink, a battalion of soldiers swept down on them. Rough hands seized their arms and legs.

"Let go!" Miriana snarled, twisting violently.

"Stop, please!" Amalia cried, her voice cracking.

Miriana wrenched a leg free and drove her heel into a guard's gut. He staggered back, but others immediately pressed in, steel ringing as blades and daggers flashed, leveled at their throats.

The soldiers then marched them through endless corridors, their boots echoing against stone. Neel, Miriana, and Amalia exchanged terrified glances, each step taking them deeper into the lion's den.

They halted at grand milky-white doors, carved with ancient sigils. The guards stationed there grimaced but pulled them open, revealing the throne room beyond.

It was vast, hung with heavy tapestries that told the kingdom's story, glowing women who seemed divine, battles won and lost, rivers of blood painted into thread. The three friends were dragged forward, up the long carpeted walk, until they were thrown down hard at the foot of the throne.

They knelt, arms now bound behind them, forced to bow their heads. Above them towered King Cedric and Queen Vivian. The king's broad figure leaned forward, his nose tilted high as though the very scent of them turned his stomach. The queen dabbed at her pale face with a cloth, her expression one of weary disgust.

"Stealing," the king muttered darkly. "Stealing from the royal family, no doubt."

The queen's cloth fluttered against her cheek. The three prisoners rolled their eyes.

"Your highness, this is a misunderstanding," Neel stammered, sweat soaking the underarms of his shirt. "We, your servants, were only cleaning your wares when we were found—"

"My servants have more loyalty than to snatch my property and hide it in a burlap sack to 'clean,'" the king hissed.

Neel's words faltered. Silence crushed them. By some cruel trick of fate, they had been caught. Now nothing remained but to kneel and await judgment.

King Cedric leaned toward his queen. Her face blanched, but she nodded gravely. His expression hardened as he straightened once more.

A single nod from him and the guards yanked at the ropes, forcing the youths lower, the cords biting into their wrists until skin scraped raw.

Miriana thrashed, trying to leap to her feet. Instantly, steel kissed her throat, three daggers pressed close enough to draw a bead of blood.

Amalia was shoved roughly to the carpet. She cried out as her chin hit stone.

"Leave her alone!" Neel shouted, his voice breaking. He spat curses at the guards until a knife pressed beneath his chin silenced him.

"QUIET!" the king roared, his voice booming through the chamber like a crack of thunder.

He glowered at them, eyes dark as storm clouds, then flicked his hand to shoo the soldiers back, but not before they shoved Neel and Miriana into the ground, joining Amalia. The youths lay sprawled on the cold floor, ropes biting their wrists.

"I am the ruler of this land," he thundered, his voice cracking through the chamber like a whip. "And I find these three guilty of treason. They shall be punished to the full extent of the law. Hanging."

All three blanched.

Amalia broke first. Tears slid down, slow at first, then faster, until her sobs rattled her whole body. She pulled against the ropes, gasping, her chest heaving in panic.

Neel went utterly pale, his arms twitching limply at his sides, his eyes fixed forward as though staring into the abyss.

Miriana's eyes widened, breath shallow, hyperventilation clawing at her lungs. A trembling hand pressed to her chest.

"No, please," Amalia whispered.

"My uncles—"

"What about our mom?"

"You can't do this!" they begged, voices overlapping, desperate.

The king snapped his fingers. Guards hauled them roughly to their feet and shoved them toward the door.

"Miriana, what are we going to do?" Amalia sobbed, her face blotched red, tear-streaks burning her cheeks. Neel said nothing, his silence heavier than a scream.

"I-I don't know," Miriana stammered. Her words cracked under the strain.

Dragged by the wrists, the three stumbled down, down, deeper into the castle's bowels. The air grew colder, the stone damp beneath their feet. Fear and chill gnawed at them equally.

At last, they reached a corridor lined with cages. One guard leaned drunkenly on his spear, drool sliding down the shaft, his stench choking the air. Another slumped asleep against the wall, reeking of stale sweat and ale.

With a squeal and clang, a cell door yawned open. Their ropes were yanked off, only for them to be shoved headlong into the darkness. The room was damp, the stone slick with mildew. No bed, no window—just a reeking bucket and two rats squealing as they darted inside it.

The stench of urine and vomit gagged Amalia. She doubled over, retching, then looked at Neel with streaming eyes before collapsing into sobs.

Neel pulled her into his arms, his own eyes brimming, though he fought to remain steady for her sake.

Miriana pressed her forehead against the rusted bars. She tried to block out the sound of her friends' despair, but guilt boiled in her chest. *I did this. I wanted to be a hero. And now, prison. Then death. For daring to want more.*

Her head drooped. If there's any plan, any chance, someone… help me. Let me protect my family. Let me make us more than this.

Behind her closed eyes, something shifted.

At first, colors swirled in the form of mere shapes, like afterimages from staring at the sun. But they sharpened. Tall, vertical. Not trees. Bars. Glowing faintly blue.

Pain throbbed behind her forehead, sharp, insistent. She clenched her teeth, unsure if she moaned aloud as the vision grew. The glow intensified. Her skull felt as if it would split. Shouts and gasps echoed around her. She wondered if they were real.

And then, silence. The pressure snapped, leaving her staggering forward.

"Miriana!" Amalia's gasp cut the air.

She turned and looked at her friends through the bars. Her friends were still in the cell, but somehow she was not.

"How did you—how did you do that?" Amalia whispered, her voice trembling with awe.

"If you could do this the entire time, why only show us now?!" Neel squawked, his fear tangled with anger.

Miriana looked down at her hands, then back at the barred gate. "Maybe the door was actually loose," she muttered weakly, clutching her forehead.

Neel grabbed the grate and shook it hard. The lock clanged, rattling, solid as iron. He and Amalia stared at her, eyes widening with dawning realization.

"You went through it," Neel said slowly. "Through a locked door. Like it was fog."

Amalia gave a small, certain nod.

"No." Miriana shook her head sharply. "That's not real. That can't happen."

"Miriana," Amalia whispered, gentling her tone, "the bars turned to smoke. I saw it."

"Hey!"

The drunken guard at the corridor's end was pointing at her, eyes bloodshot and furious.

Miriana froze. If I can get them out, there'll be time to throw up later. Not now.

"Miriana!" the twins shouted in unison. "You have to get out of here!"

She spun, her heart racing. "I'll be back for you both!" she called.

The guards stirred—the drunk one bellowing, the other groaning awake.

Miriana leapt, her boots striking stone. She vaulted over the drunk guard, heel smashing against his jaw. He collapsed with a grunt. She dashed into a chamber that led to a spiraling stair.

The second guard hurled his spear. It whistled through the air and struck, burying itself into her arm.

Pain exploded. Miriana screamed, stumbling. The guard tackled her, his hand twisting in her hair as he slammed her head into the stone floor again and again. Blood spattered across the ground. Her nose cracked with the impact.

He yanked her head up high, ready for the killing blow.

With a guttural cry, she wrenched the spear from her arm and rammed it into his.

He shrieked, collapsing. Miriana staggered free, sprinting up the stair. She didn't stop until she reached a landing high above.

Breath ragged, she pressed her sleeve to her bloodied face. Her nose throbbed, crooked. With shaking fingers, she snapped it back into place, biting down on a groan. Tearing her sleeves, she wrapped one strip around her head and the other around her arm to staunch the bleeding.

She pressed on, climbing. Voices echoed ahead. She slowed, crept closer, and ripped an empty torch from the wall.

When the guard turned, she swung with all her strength. The torch cracked against his skull, and he crumpled to the floor.

Miriana sagged against the opposite wall, chest heaving, body trembling with exhaustion. Her eyes drifted to the fallen man's cloak. She pulled it from his body and draped it over herself, the hood shadowing her face.

In the disguise, she slipped into the winding halls, each step driving her toward one goal: finding the guard who had taken her sword.

CHAPTER SIX

The gallows had been built high, towering above the crowd so that the sickened public could savor their gruesome spectacle. The town square was packed, shoulder to shoulder, a restless sea of faces. Three ropes swayed in the late wind, creaking faintly against the wooden beams.

A thin whimper broke the air. Two beaten figures stood before the crowd, their ragged clothing now replaced with the ropes that awaited them. Their swollen faces spoke of interrogation, of questions demanded over and over. The whereabouts of the third had been pressed from them, yet none of their desperate answers proved satisfactory.

They were shoved forward, stumbling as they dragged their broken bodies and fading fight.

"Please!" one cried, his voice cracking.

"Please, we were just hungry!"

"We only wanted to feed our families!" they begged, their voices tripping over one another. But their pleas fell like stones into a pit. Rough hands forced them up the stairs, onto the barrels that rocked slightly under their weight.

Neel's cheeks were wet with tears, his small frame trembling. Beside him, Amalia stood stiff, her silence sharper than any cry, her eyes fixed on the ever-thickening crowd. The people watched with anticipatory ears and curious eyes. Executions were rare, and that rarity made the morbid gathering even thicker with tension and hotter with suspense. Everyone's eyes were so focused on the rare occasion that no one noticed the cloaked figure crouched on the roofline of a nearby building.

Miriana.

Her breath came quick, fogging in the night as she darted across the tiles. She leapt from roof to roof, cloak snapping behind her, shadows swallowing her every move.

"The two before you," the executioner declared, his gravelly voice carrying over the heads of the crowd, "have been tried with thievery and high treason. Yet a third is missing. We will find you! You hear, you will never rest safely!"

Miriana slowed at the edge of a bakery roof, peering down. Her friends stood helpless, nooses brushing their necks as the executioner droned on, weighting crimes like stones on a scale. The crowd grew restless, buzzing with the cruel anticipation of the drop.

Sliding down the wooden frame of the building, Miriana moved with the ease and years of experience of climbing. The years spent scaling her uncles' tree had hardened her hands and, she thought bitterly, made her the nimble thief she was now.

Her boots touched the cobblestones, and she melted into shadow. A quick dart through the press of people brought her to the stage. She spotted a gap in the boards beneath the platform and squeezed through, her slight frame slipping into the dark hollow under her friends' feet.

"Now what?" she muttered under her breath. Her heart hammered. She had never stormed an execution before. Above, the executioner raised his leg onto the crate Amalia was standing on. He drew out the moment, the hush deepening as the crowd leaned closer, as if the entire kingdom of Sorcerac were watching.

Amalia stood pale as snow, beads of sweat plastering her dark hair to her cheeks.

Think, think, think, Miriana panicked.

Miriana's eyes flicked across the square, across the crowd, the roofs, the soldiers. And there! A thin rope dangled loose, leading up to the platform. Without hesitation, she seized it, muscles burning as she climbed. Her braid slipped loose, strands clinging to her damp face; her cloak tangled around her legs, suffocating, but she didn't stop.

She pulled herself onto the stage. In one fluid motion, she swung the rope, vaulting up. Gasps rippled through the people. All eyes turned as her navy cape unfurled like a banner against the sky.

"There!" voices shouted. "The third one!"

The executioner sneered, lowering his leg with deliberate slowness. "Well, my people," he bellowed, "it seems the third thief has chosen to reveal themselves."

He bent, sliding a dagger from his boot. His charge was sudden, steel flashing.

Miriana ripped off her cloak, flinging it into his path. It wrapped around his head, smothering him in fabric. She leapt onto his back, twisting, pulling the cloth tighter. The man cursed, tugging at the cape while trying to avoid his blade. When his hand rose again, she lunged forward and sank her teeth into his wrist. Hot, metallic blood filled her mouth, and he howled, staggering.

She spat, wiped her mouth, jumped down, and bolted across the gallows.

"Hold on!" she hissed, leaping onto Amalia's barrel. The wood rocked precariously beneath them both. Her fingers worked frantically at the knot of the noose.

"Miriana—" Amalia's voice cracked. Miriana turned around to see the bowling soldiers approaching.

"Be right back," Miriana breathed, eyes darting toward the charging guards.

"What?!" Amalia's cry broke against the roar of the crowd.

"Miriana!" Neel's desperate shout stabbed through the chaos.

But she was already moving, steel escaping from its sheath. She met the guards with a flurry of strikes, her blade flashing like silver lightning. The clash of iron filled the square. She ducked low, springing from her back in a swift kick that knocked a soldier's weapon clear. She flipped, landed hard, blade raised in defiance. The soldier scrambled for their fallen sword.

This is going to be fun, she thought grimly.

Her strike dented a guard's armor with a slash of her blade. He countered by bringing down his sword onto hers, sending sparks into their faces. She twisted, swiping her leg under his, throwing him flat on his back. Rolling onto her shoulder, she snatched her sword again and whirled to cut through the ropes binding her friends. She ran and with a slash, severed their nooses into necklaces. Her friends removed them from their necks.

"Run through the crowd!" she ordered, helping Neel stumble free. "The soldiers won't risk casualties. They'll never cut through fast enough!"

"Stop! In the name of the king!" a soldier thundered before lunging at them.

"Now! Head to my uncle's --"

"Tavern!" Neel and Amalia chorused, as though the word had been stitched into their bones.

Together, the three leapt from the stage. The crowd shrank back, muttering, gasping as they tumbled past, rolling and slipping between startled townsfolk.

Behind them, soldiers fought against the wall of bodies, their pursuit slowed by the crush of human force.

Miriana, Amalia, and Neel burst through the tavern doors and slammed them shut, the din of the square still rattling at their backs.

"Can we hide in the apartments in the back?" Amalia asked as her brother shoved a table and a couple of chairs against the battered tavern doors. It was the slow hour; the common room was mercifully near empty, the hearth just a dull glow instead of a roar. Miriana moved from window to window like a restless sentry, studying the square, reading the motion of helmets and cloaks beyond the glass.

Someone cleared his throat behind them.

Igneus and Valcom leaned against the bar with authority. Their arms were crossed and they raised their eyebrows, ready for answers.

"I'm assuming your parents don't even know where you were today. Or any other day?" Valcom pressed, voice as blunt as a dead end.

"Well—" Neel started, then fell silent when Igneus lifted a hand, stopping the excuse before it could form.

"Did you hear, Valcom, that there was to be a hanging today in the square? One was said to try to end the execution and wearing a cloak that our very own Miriana is wearing just now!" Igneus said, amusement curling the edge of his words.

Heat crept up Miriana's neck; she slipped the cloak from her shoulders and let it pool at her feet. Valcom exhaled.

"Yes, I did," he said. "Thank goodness they escaped. Can you imagine how angry the families would be if their kin were foolish enough to get caught?" His tone was chastising and oddly proud at once.

"Uncles—" Miriana began, but the words were swallowed as both men closed on her in a sudden, dry embrace that smelled faintly of beer and salt.

"We never really had a family until your parents gave you up," Valcom grunted into her hair. "If you dare act so carelessly with your life again, I swear I will tie you to the boards of this tavern myself." The threat was as much affection as warning.

"Alright," Miriana said, the single syllable softening the rebuke. The twins hovered by the door, awkward and small.

"Are you going to get caught again?" Igneus prodded, releasing his niece with a theatrical shove.

"Absolutely not," Miriana replied, chin lifted.

"No, sir," Neel stammered.

"Then I see no need to tell your parents if you don't mention what I do to them," Igneus said, shrugging as if the fate of three children could be contained in a promise. "Now, excuse me all, but I have an appointment." He moved toward the door.

"An 'appointment?' I thought you were not going to go through with this one," Valcom snorted, following.

"This one pays exceedingly well. I would never need to continue these errands again," Igneus explained, voice low with a greedy gleam.

"And what of the island afterward?" Valcom asked.

Igneus threaded himself between the twins, shoulder brushing theirs as he pushed toward the threshold. "What has it done for us?" he asked, letting the weight of the question hang as the heavy doors thudded shut behind him.

***

Neel walked around the Ele tree, dragging his hand across the grain of the acquired wood for their own fortress.

"Do you think Princess Juliet appreciates mahogany?" he gushed, fingers tracing the grain as if it might answer him.

"She's royalty. She doesn't care," Amalia replied, exasperated but fond. "*Where is Miriana?*"

"Right behind you." They turned and found her in simpler clothes, a blue long-sleeved shirt and red trousers that were patched at the knee, the colors the way she usually wore them. The small birthmark near her temple, a dab of darker pigment that looked as if the heavens had spat a single drop of ink on her face, seemed to catch the spring sun and glow. Her braid fell like a rope down her back. In one hand, she held a rolled parchment; the other rested on her hip, as if she were balancing plans and temper in equal measure. Her sword in its home scabbard.

"What's that?" Amalia asked, nodding toward the paper.

"Oh no," Neel sighed.

Miriana ignored him. She climbed the scaffolding of the half-finished deck, slipping up with the easy grace of someone who had spent a childhood in branches. She tucked the roll between her teeth to keep it from falling and then, with a flourish, spread the parchment across the rough wood. Amalia and Neel scrambled up beside her.

"I did some staking, and this is what I came up with," Miriana said, fingers tapping the crude drawings.

"While I was working my ass off," Neel scoffed, though his tone had the wry edge of one who couldn't help but admire the audacity.

"While you were hoping for Juliet," Amalia teased.

Miriana pointed. "The windows lining the hall of the palace are about five feet off the floor and three feet across. It'll be a squeeze." On the paper, a rough sketch of the castle's facade showed little stick-figure guards, arrows to indicate sightlines, and notes about when the watch rotated. They were sitting on the planks of Miriana's platform, the wood warm from the sun and creaking slightly under their weight.

"One final heist," Neel said, trying to sound brave. "We'll have enough to live off for a while before we start 'hero-ing.'" He flattened the last word with disdain; the idea of parading about as champions seemed, to him, both risky and naive.

"We're going to stop my uncle from killing the king and queen. We're going to save the kingdom," Miriana said, her voice steady and fierce. Her eyes flared like flint. "So we can save our families. The island. So we can have a future. Don't you want that? Don't you want to help your mother?"

Neel and Amalia both looked away, the truth in her question a bright, painful thing. They shuffled on the plank, avoiding the eyes that demanded an answer and offered none.

"How are we going to do that?" Amalia whispered, doubt braided through the softness of her voice.

"I overheard my uncles. He's going to do it today." Miriana traced the guard rotations. "We're going to infiltrate the castle, find crown jewels to set us up for life, find Igneus, and save the king and queen. I have a plan."

Neel folded his arms, "I just think it would be more effort than it's worth. You save someone, and everyone can just assume you were part of the plot, and the next thing you know, you're dead in an execution. People turn fast. It sounds painful, and luckily, it's an avoidable mess."

"Everyone was mad when they discovered their belongings had disappeared too," Amalia pointed out. Neel's shoulders sagged in defeat.

Miriana raised an eyebrow at both of them, half amusement, half command, and their bickering died as if the wind had taken the spark. They sat a long moment in the sunlight, the plan between them like a small, fragile thing that might either lift them or break them.

"Right, so as I was saying," Miriana continued, tapping the parchment with the back of her knuckle, "the windows that line the hall are going to be a tight fit. Either we rule that out, or Amalia sneaks through them alone, gets the keys for the cellar doors, and we all slip inside the castle from there. Thoughts?"

Neel's eyes widened in horror, mirrored perfectly by Amalia's—though hers gleamed with something closer to excitement.

"You want me to send my little sister into the castle by herself?" Neel gaped. "With even more guards than usual? Just so she can let us in? And that's only the first part of your plan?"

Amalia's lips curved. "One, I can handle myself. Two, I'm in."

"What?!" Neel's voice cracked.

"Neel, it's my chance to do something important. Something real. Something big for the team."

"You were always against stealing!"

Amalia's gaze was steady. "If we're going to be heroes, and no one in this world will give two bards and a swordswoman a job, then we need funds. And I'm willing to put in the effort. Are you?"

Neel flailed his arms, gesturing at Amalia as if her words were flies he could bat away. His eyes begged Miriana for sense, for an ally.

But Miriana only folded her arms. "Sorry, Neel, but it's her choice. If it'll make you feel better, we can put it to a vote."

Amalia's grin was radiant. Neel's expression darkened, like clouds rolling in.

"For me to be my own hero," Amalia declared, raising her hand. Miriana joined her without hesitation.

"All opposed?"

Neel thrust his arm skyward, waving it frantically. "Me! Definitely me! This is insanity!"

"Sorry, Neel," Amalia teased, victory lighting her eyes. "Looks like I'm going in. How far from the ground are the windows?"

"At least fifteen feet," Miriana estimated, squinting as though measuring in her mind.

Neel clutched his hair. "You mean you don't know for sure?! How is she even supposed to get up there?! *Fly?!*"

Amalia placed a calming hand on his knee. "We'll find rope, brother."

"And we'll practice," Miriana added smoothly. "Climbing, sneaking, everything we can do to make it run as clean as possible. Besides, Neel, this isn't the first time we've done something ridiculous."

"I know," he groaned, "but this time it's my sister risking her life."

The days that followed were a blur of stolen hours. They filched rope from a nearby farm and tied it to the highest branches of the Ele's tree. Over and over, Amalia climbed, fell, scraped her hands raw, then climbed again. Each time, her movements grew quicker, quieter, surer. By the end of two weeks, she could slide to the top without sound, like a shadow dressed in spring sunlight.

At last, the three crouched in the brush outside the castle walls, cloaked by the thick greenery. The looming stone towered above, its window a black square fifteen feet up.

"Does everybody know what they're doing?" Miriana whispered. Her voice carried authority but also the weight of her own nerves.

Amalia gave a sharp, eager nod. Neel's scowl could have soured wine.

"Don't be such a sourpuss," Amalia murmured, elbowing him. Her smile coaxed a reluctant twitch of his lips, more for her sake than from any true amusement.

Miriana took their makeshift grappling hook, a bundle of fused horseshoes lashed to a coarse rope, and swung it high. It clanged against the wall, then lodged inside the sill with a crash that shattered the glass.

The three froze, hearts thundering, waiting for shouts, an alarm.

"…Odd," Neel remarked.

"They could be in a meeting," Amalia reasoned, eyes scanning the courtyard. "Or the guards could all be patrolling. Or maybe everyone's enjoying the weather."

"Alright, alright, stop guessing," Neel muttered, rolling his eyes.

Miriana tugged sharply on the rope. It held. "Safe," she whispered.

Amalia hugged her brother quickly, tightly. "See you on the other side."

"Amalia—"

But she was already shimmying up the rope, skirts brushing the stone. She slid through the broken window with the grace of practice, waving once before tossing the hook back down.

Neel seized Miriana by the shoulders and spun her toward him. His face was pale, eyes hard. "If anything—*anything*—happens to my sister, Miriana, I swear—"

"On the supreme off-chance that anything does," Miriana cut in, laying a hand over her chest, "I'll throw myself off the tower. You have my word."

His glare held, but he let her go.

Inside, Amalia landed softly on the polished stone floor. She was wearing a simple pastel dress that had been borrowed and altered to look noble enough. She pressed to the wall, moving from shadow to shadow, heart pounding at every sound.

Rounding a corner, she nearly collided with an older man in a dark brown petticoat, ruffled shirt puffing beneath his chin, boots clicking sharply on the floor. His lined face was pinched with cuts from a past fight, fading into scars and bruises. His voice sharp as a frog's rasp when it lashed out:

"You there! Why are you gawking about?"

Amalia froze. *Cecil.* The steward.

" I-I'm from here," she stammered, cursing herself instantly, "What are you doing?" She could have smacked her forehead—of course, he knew who she was. And of course, fate would throw *him* in her path. He had mocked her and her brother when they'd once lingered near the castle kitchens, and time had only soured his expression.

"I am the king's steward, you idiot," he snapped. "His right hand. You were excused from duties, I believe. What are you doing back here?"

Her heart sank. His words confirmed everything.

Think fast.

In a voice far louder and sharper than her own, she burst out: "I am the princess's lady-in-waiting, you blathering buttress! I was searching for the keys to the cellar to procure her majesty's cranberry preserves. I take my duties to the throne very seriously. There is no end to my loyalty. And I was *gawking*, as you put it, only because you've distracted me from them!"

Her words spilled like fire, her chin high as she jabbed a finger at him. "Cecil, I've always taken pride in my work, and I will not fail now. Give me the keys!"

The steward staggered back a step, his bluster collapsing into stammers. Then, narrowing his eyes, he fixed her with a long, suspicious look.

"She—" the steward began, then faltered. "Her majesty is allergic to cranberries."

Shit, Amalia thought. *If I'm already in a hole, might as well keep digging.*

She stepped closer, chin high, pressing his small chest with a single accusing finger. Reaching the very tips of her toes, she lowered her voice into its grandest, most pompous register.

"I said, *raspberry*, you clown," she declared, venom sweetened by theatrics. "Now, if you have the keys, I would love to have them. Otherwise, I shall go and inform Her Majesty that some *selfish* ninny would deny the *princess* her royal treat. Shall I tell her that?"

The steward's face went from indignation to panic in a heartbeat. "No-n-no, ma'am." He fumbled at his waist and drew the keys out as if they were a hot coal, thrusting them at her with shaking hands.

"Thank you." Amalia bowed with exaggerated grace, the hem of her pastel dress flashing a glimpse of dusty, clumpy boots. "I'll be sure to put in a good word for you to the royal family," she added, teeth bared in a smile that was all teeth and no warmth, then she pivoted and ran down the corridor.

As she hurried, the tapestries and portraits of long-dead monarchs looked stern and judge-like, their painted eyes tracking her. The plush carpet swallowed her footsteps, and for a dizzy second, she let herself imagine *living* beneath those vaulted ceilings. *I wouldn't mind this,* she thought, then shook herself back to the task.

At the end of the corridor stood a single cream-colored door. She fitted the key into the lock, turned it with a sharp twist, and the latch clicked. The door swung inward on a hiss of stale air.

The cellar reeked of damp and old wood. Cobwebs hung like chandeliers in the corners, and dusty barrel stacks rose in columns to the low ceiling. Near the far wall, a short flight of stone steps led to a heavy plank that, if she strained her ears, muffled the life outside the castle.

Amalia crept to the steps and pressed her ear to the splintering wood. "Miriana? Neel? You there?" she whispered.

"Yeah. Open the door," Neel's urgent voice leaked through.

She swung the door wide. Miriana and Neel toppled into the cellar in a tumble of limbs, sending Amalia sprawling onto the cold floor. She laughed, breathless.

"You two didn't need to lean against it. I was coming—so eager." Her words were mocking, warm.

Neel sprang up, dusting himself off, and offered a callused hand to help his sister up. She accepted it, smiling with a flash of triumph.

"Well, we weren't sure with how long you took," he jibed, though the relief on his face belied the teasing.

Miriana stretched and surveyed the low-ceilinged room. "Alright. Onward to the crown jewels," she said, voice steady and business-like. They moved quickly, slipping from shadow to shadow.

"Ran into Cecil," Amalia warned. "Think he's onto me."

Neel's jaw tightened; he shot Miriana a look that said, *Told you so.* Miriana ignored the reproach, eyes already on the map in her mind.

"We'll deal with him if we must," Miriana said. "Where are the crowns kept?"

"Rumor among the guards is there's a hidden room beneath the thrones," Neel panted, and they set off with renewed speed.

Outside, under the cover of dusk, other shapes were moving less cautiously, but more deadly. Shadows eased through the filth of a grated sewer and spilled into the castle's underbelly.

"We have been betrayed by our brother," a hard voice hissed. "He has taken a vow and deceived us. He plans to fight against us to protect those that he was tasked to deal with." Angry mutterings and yells filled the quiet.

"We will finish the task he failed," he continued.

What followed was a swift, brutal betrayal of order. Men, familiar with knives and with merciless intent, slipped through blind spots and down service corridors. Where they found soldiers too tired or too slow to defend themselves, they struck without mercy, using the defenders' own blades against them. They crawled through windows, smashed down doors, and filled the castle like an infestation.

Panic erupted. Staff scattered. Maids cowering in corners, butlers and cooks scrambling with pans and ladles that did little against the flash of steel. Screams ricocheted off stone as the invaders stalked the halls and carried out swift, savage brutality.

"Good work, men!" Romof roared over the chaos, his voice a trumpet of cruelty. "They thought there were only a few of us. But we are like ants; see one, and there are hundreds more!" The shout was met with a savage cheer that echoed through the vaulted corridors, a sound like triumph and a storm.

At the tavern, Valcom paced the floor in an anxious loop, head bent low beneath the dim light. "He could not have left. He's not actually going to—" He muttered the sentence to himself and to the empty room, the worry making his hands twitch.

He had barred the doors and shut the bar early, an act of denial as much as protection. The hours dragged. The tavern felt hollow, like a ship abandoned at sea. He could not sit and wait any longer. Grief and fear braided into resolve; he would intercept his brother, stop whatever madness was set in motion. With his coat thrown tight around him, Valcom set off into the night, footsteps biting into the cold as he made for the castle, intent on preventing the worst. Or dying trying.

Valcom shrugged his moth-eaten cloak about his shoulders, the same thin thing that doubled as a blanket on his bed, and shoved his feet into shoes that had seen better winters. He told himself he was leaving the choice to Igneus; his brother was an adult, after all. That he wasn't at the castle, but at the market. But what if? How could a man choose a path that would rip the family apart? How could a man be so blind?

His plan was less a plan and more a string of desperate hopes: sneak into the castle, find his brother, convince him to stop. That was it. Nothing elegant, nothing clever. He snorted at himself as he latched the tavern door behind him.

You are a runt. You are nothing. You and your brother are the fungus that poisons the family tree. You will drag Simon down.

The old taunts of his parents crawled back into his head like winter insects. He pulled the cloak tighter and shoved the thoughts away with every step toward the palace. People glanced at him as he passed, and he imagined their curious and contemptuous whispers were all aimed at him. He felt small and useless, a man who wallowed in mud while others climbed.

No, he countered, more to himself than to anyone else. *They don't know. They can't feel what I feel.*

The fortress loomed above him, black and indifferent against the night. He kept his gaze low; the cobbles bit at the soles of his shoes as though testing his resolve. *God, what are you doing, Igneus?* he wondered with a bitterness that pricked like nettles.

At the outer gate, a small procession of farmers pulled a creaking cart into the court. Valcom fell in behind them, close enough to blend but careful to avoid drawing notice. A guard, broad-shouldered and hooded in a metal helm that made his face a shadow, stepped up to inspect the approaching party. Valcom's heart thudded against his ribs like a trapped thing.

"We've come to implore their Highnesses for more tools for the fish market," the farmer said, his voice steady enough though his clothes were rough. Valcom watched the guard circle the wagon, peering at its contents and at the faces of those who rode with it.

The guard stopped a breath away from Valcom, the spear he carried bristling like an accusation. Valcom felt its chill in his thoughts.

"Alright," the soldier finally said, voice flat. "You may enter." He signaled to the tower, and with a grinding clatter, the gate lifted. The small group flowed into the courtyard; Valcom shrank under the sweep of lords and ladies moving past in their finery, the perfume and silk of them a world he was not part of.

Up close, the fortress felt even more implacable. Stone rose in tiers, and banners stirred in the high wind, the royal sigil a constant reminder of power he had no right to touch. Valcom broke away from the group when he saw a side door to the cellars left ajar. It was an invitation he could not refuse.

He slipped through the gap and shut the door behind him with a soft push. The cellar smelled of old ale, salt, and damp, stale, but alive with activity. He hurried through the passage, keeping to the shadows, the coarse air stinging his lungs when he took it in. At the end of the corridor, a heavy wooden door led into the castle proper; he heaved it open and spilled into the hall beyond.

He ran then, heedless of where his feet took him, ignoring the clatter of armor and the distant, mounting cries that had begun to thread through the night. His breath came sharp and ragged; the pulse at his throat was a drumbeat of fear and hope braided together.

Rounding a corner, he heard the chaos ahead: frantic shouts, armor clashing, the harsh bark of commanders over the din, and beneath it all, the unmistakable clangor and shout of battle spilling into marble halls. He slowed, pressed himself to the dark, and peered around a column. Beyond a pair of tall white doors rimmed in gold, the great *throne room* spanned wide. Voices rose like a storm within.

Valcom eased the doors open a fraction and slipped inside, ducking along the wall to melt into the shadows. He flattened himself close to the wall, every muscle ready, every sense alert, as the tumult of the night rolled on.

CHAPTER SEVEN

Igneus's boots struck the marble floor like thunder, each step ricocheting down the cavernous hallways of the castle. The walls were tall, cold, and pale, flanked with identical doors that blurred together until his breath grew tight in his chest. Somewhere beyond one of those doors lay the royal chamber. Somewhere, his quarry.

Shadows shifted with the flicker of wall sconces, their flames hissing against dripping wax. From around the bend came the hushed murmur of voices. He could sense the guards patrolling. Igneus froze. The whispers sharpened into the clipped cadence of soldiers, boots echoing in unison. He searched for escape, and his gaze caught on the first door ajar. He slipped silently inside.

The chamber welcomed him with oppressive silence. Satin sheets gleamed in the dim candlelight, spread neatly across a bed wide enough for three men. Plump pillows lay arranged like offerings on the dandelion-colored coverlet. Above it hung a painted portrait: the royal family, stiffly posed. A queen in flowing emerald, a king draped in blue, and a girl perched uneasily upon her father's lap in a golden dress. None smiled. Their painted eyes seemed to follow him with disapproval.

He ducked toward a hulking wardrobe of dark, polished oak. The doors creaked faintly as he eased one open and slipped inside, the scent of cedar and old fabric thick in his lungs. He pressed the door nearly shut, crouched among gowns and cloaks, and waited.

Time slowed, stretching taut until his muscles ached from stillness. Then... heels clicking, a door flung wide, and voices like clashing steel.

"No, Vivian, I do not understand what has become of Juliet. She is just a child!" A man's voice, gravelly with authority but edged with frustration.

"Now she hides herself away, silent, skirting courtiers, skulking off like a—"

"And what?" he cut her off sharply. "What treachery do you suspect in our daughter now?"

"Cedric," the queen's reply poured into the room like music, low and pleading, "perhaps what she needs is change. The castle grows... suffocating."

"Suffocating?" Cedric's voice snapped like a whip.

"Cedric," she whispered, "you know our marriage was arranged." There is a lot of pressure of being that young with all those decisions.

A pause. The scrape of boots against stone. Then, softer: the king stepped closer. Igneus, peering through the wardrobe's sliver, caught sight of him at last; a tall, broad-shouldered man, though the years had traced frost into his beard. He reached for his queen's hand, lowering his head in a gesture of weary humility.

"Vivian... I pray love has begun to grow between us. But I confess that this cursed isle has driven me to madness. No one taught me how to rule. It was thrust upon me. I've failed you. But if you could... guide me, show me mercy. I would be grateful."

Her lips trembled into a smile. "Oh, Cedric. You've never asked for help before. Perhaps this is a change for the better, hm?" She leaned forward, pressing a gentle kiss to his cheek.

Igneus rolled his eyes in the dark and let out the faintest scoff. *Enough.*

He burst from the wardrobe in a swift movement, steel rasping as his blade sang free.

"How touching," he sneered, eyes glinting. He angled his sword toward them.

"Now, be very still while I take your lives. No one is coming for you and no one will hear you."

Queen Vivian shrieked, stumbling back.

"Guar—!" King Cedric's bellow was strangled into silence as Igneus pressed the blade against his throat, the cold steel kissing flesh. Igneus flicked his gaze to the queen and lifted a finger to his lips. The gesture was calm, almost mocking. Terrified, Vivian slapped both hands over her mouth, swaying as if her knees might give way.

Impatience twitched through Igneus's limbs; he bounced lightly on the balls of his feet. With a flick of his dagger, he motioned them apart, king to one side, queen to the other, reasoning neither could save the other in time. A churn of unease rolled in his stomach. He smothered it.

"Your Majesties," he drawled, "there are those displeased with your rule. I've come to remedy that… permanently."

"Where are the guards?" the queen whispered, her voice thin as paper.

"They won't be troubling us," Igneus growled, lips curling.

The royal couple stared at one another from across the room, whispering hurried fragments of sentences as if the other could hear. Remembrances, regrets, last words left unsaid too long. Igneus raised his blade high above the king, every nerve pulsating. His mind burned with one choice, one decision.

He lunged.

But the door crashed open before the strike could fall.

A sharp cry rang through the chamber.

Miriana stood frozen on the threshold, hand still on the door handle, her face drained of color. Her mouth hung open, disbelief and horror mingling in her eyes.

"Uncle… what are you doing? You said ---" she quavered , the last of her sentence falling off.

"Miriana…" In that split second, the king wrestles the sword away and puts it to Igneus's neck, applying extreme pressure. Blood begins to trickle down Igneus's nape and onto the sword. Vivian runs to the door and tries to shield Miriana.

"Hey, move! That's my uncle!"

"What?" the king and queen choked.

"Oh, Miriana," Igneus groaned, trying to wrestle with the sword.

"You were really gonna go through with it?! What about Valcom!? What about me!? Are the riches…they aren't worth a life. What the hell?" Miriana hissed. She finally allowed herself to admit what she has always truly known, "The riches aren't going–they're not worth it."

Igneus looked away in shame.

Miriana pushes the queen out of the way and begins to unsheathe her sword. She runs up to the bed with the sword raised at the king.

"Miriana, no!!!" The scream was barely audible over the roar of the blades. The king shoved Igneus to the ground with a grunt. He then jumped down and lunged at Miriana. She spun around, sword raised high, and slashed at the king. Sparks flew from the clash of the blades. They charged at each other, trying to unbalance one another. Igneus stood up and ran to wrest the sword from Miriana. The queen had long since fainted, trembling, but no one paid attention.

Miriana leapt into the air, missing Igneus, and drove her sword downward. Igneus fell to the floor with a thud, then turned around to assess his options. The king, startled, fell back and rolled out of the aim. Miriana landed and rolled toward him; she brought herself up to a kneeling position and pressed the edge of her sword under King Cedric's chin. He raised his sword to her neck.

"Yield," she panted.

"I'm a king, *child.* I yield to no one," he spat. Miriana was about to sneer a response when Igneus stole the sword out of the king's hand.

"Go home, Miriana. I took an oath. I've been branded. I have to be here," Igneus stood up, grabbing the king by his collar and thrusting him to the floor next to his wife.

Miriana stood up and held her sword out in front of her. An extension of herself, just like her mentor taught her. Her mentor, a few feet in front of her, with his arms raised, kept his face neutral.

"You're still going through with it. You're going to ruin everyone's life, casting Sorcerac into chaos and destruction," she shook her head. She sidestepped in front of the door.

"Miriana, you don't understand. I need to do this. For everyone," Igneus scowled.

"I can't let you do this."

Igneus took a step toward her, his boots clicking against the stone floor, echoing around the growing silent room. The king grabs his wife and tries to move out the door. Igneus wags his finger at him, not taking his eyes off his niece.

"It's not worth it," Miriana mutters.

Igneus' demeanor changed. His face showed his fury, and he lowered his hands. With the sword, he lunged at Miriana, who parried the attack. She swung toward him, but he jumped back, flipping the sword over in his hand. He parried, his sword slicing through the air, just inches from his niece's face. She rolled onto her shoulder beneath his blade.

Miriana landed light as a cat, knees bending to absorb the impact. She feigned an advance, steel flashing forward. Igneus braced, raising his sword across his chest, only for her blade to curl like a whip around his, wrenching it from his grip. His weapon spun skyward, clattering onto the marble floor.

For a heartbeat, their eyes locked. Uncle and niece, attacker and protector. Neither blinked.

Then Igneus surged, boot lashing out to kick her weapon high. He leapt, snatching it midair in a fluid arc, spinning to strike. The air hissed as the blade carved toward her.

Miriana dove for his fallen sword. Her fingers closed around the hilt; she rose just as Igneus pivoted. Steel clashed against steel in a shower of sparks. She twisted her wrist, catching his strike on the cross-guard and whipping her blade down hard. His sword slipped from his grip, flying toward him, almost as though she had thrown it back. Igneus caught it mid-spin with a snarl, lunging forward in one swift motion.

Miriana sidestepped, instincts driving her hand to thrust. The blade met flesh.

A gasp split the room. The sound seemed to echo endlessly.

Her uncle's eyes widened as scarlet blood seeped across his thigh. Blood poured down his leg, splashing across marble, seeping into cracks like vines. He staggered, collapsing to one knee.

Miriana's face drained of color. Her sword was slick and trembling in her hands as horror wracked her chest. With a cry that was half sob, half scream, she flung the weapon aside, its clatter ringing louder than thunder.

"Uncle…" Her knees buckled as she crawled toward him. "I'm sorry, I didn't… If I hadn't… You would've, *could've* been killed. Oh god, I'm so sorry!" Her shaking hands tore the silken blankets from the bed, pressing the fabric desperately to the wound.

"Igneus!"

The cry came from the doorway. A group of men stormed into the chamber, their faces shadowed, their leather stained, and their weapons bristling. Leading them was a man scarred beyond recognition, his pale stubble giving him a carved-from-stone appearance. His eyes, black with fury, locked onto Igneus.

"Traitor!" Romof roared, yanking a knife free of his belt.

Miriana stumbled up, steel half-drawn once more, but her foot caught on the edge of the carpet. She crashed to her knees, panic setting into her lungs. Above her, Igneus's gaze flicked from his niece to the advancing men.

His mouth curled into a lopsided grin. "Not today, kid."

He jerked his chin toward Neel and Amalia, who had appeared in the doorway behind her. They had been following her since she had heard shouting.

"Get her out of here."

"What—?" Miriana choked, but already the twins seized her under the arms, hauling her up against her thrashing resistance.

Igneus was already moving, blood trailing his steps. With a guttural roar, he launched himself at the intruders.

"They're swarming around him," Miriana gasped, struggling in her friends' grip, "they'll kill him."

"Go!" Igneus barked, hurling a knife across the hall. It buried itself deep in a man's thigh. The man howled, ripping it free with blood-slick fingers.

Amalia and Neel dragged Miriana backward, her heels scraping uselessly against the marble. She could only watch in dumbstricken shock, heartbroken, as the tide of bodies swallowed her uncle.

Igneus fought like a man possessed. His fist cracked against a jaw, a sickening snap as bone gave way. A body fell limp. But another attacker looped an arm around his neck, yanking him back into a chokehold.

Igneus staggered, his throat compressed, the grip tightening like a noose of flesh. Others surged in, fists pummeling his ribs, driving air and strength from him He tried to kick, to find a way to stand completely up, but a sharp jab of pain made him trip.

He thrashed, his vision swimming, torn between clawing at the iron arm, choking him and reaching for the daggers strapped at his belt. His body spasmed under each brutal blow. Pain seared through his chest, hot and blinding. His knees finally buckled; the world blurred.

And then the mob parted.

Romof stepped forward, moving leisurely, slicing through his own men as if they were air. His scarred face twisted in a sneer as he seized Igneus's tunic, yanking it down to bare the branded mark on his chest.

"Tsk, tsk." His voice dripped with contempt. "Loyalty." He spat the word like poison. "A thief even among your kin. You betray your own blood, and for what?"

He plucked a dagger from Igneus's belt, weighing it in his scarred hands as though savoring the irony. His smile spread, crooked and cruel.

"You never had foresight, brother," Romof hissed. "I can fix that."

The knife touched Igneus's forehead, cold and merciless. Slowly, Romof dragged it down, carving from hairline toward the eye. Igneus writhed, teeth grinding as blood flooded his vision. His sky-blue eye turned crimson.

Romof pressed the blade deeper, pushing into the soft flesh of the eyelid. Igneus's scream tore through the chamber, raw and animal.

A wet, hideous *pop*.

The world spun scarlet. His tunic was drenched, his face a mask of blood. The crowd released him, and he crumpled to the marble. His eye fell from him, rolling with a grotesque bounce until it landed in front of his cheek.

Romof loomed over him, laughter rasping in his throat. He drove a savage kick into Igneus's gut, forcing blood to bubble up and spill from his lips.

"I leave you a mark," Romof declared, stepping back as his men withdrew. "Remember it. Remember the family you chose... and betrayed."

Their footsteps thundered away, leaving silence and the reek of iron.

Igneus lay sprawled in the blood pooling around his skull, his remaining eye drifting shut.

He did not know how much time had passed before a voice pierced the void.

"Oh god!"

He forced his eye open, the world swimming in watery light. Valcom knelt over him, pale and trembling, hands hovering as if afraid to touch.

"Valcom?" Igneus rasped, his throat raw.

He tried to rise but collapsed into a fit of wet coughing. Valcom gently eased him back down. His brother's face was white as parchment, his hand shaking against his mouth.

"I... I came to stop you," Valcom stammered. "From doing… from doing it. Oh god…" His voice cracked, nearly breaking.

He tore a strip from his worn brown shirt, pressing it against the ruin of Igneus's socket with shaky hands. Igneus turned his head away, as though even his brother's pity was unbearable. His gaze fixed on the floor… and the orb lying there, reflecting him.

His eye.

"Foresight," he whispered hoarsely, his lips curling into a broken laugh.

"Foresight," he repeated, louder now, until his voice dissolved into wild cackling. "It's so small!"

Valcom's grimace deepened. He cupped Igneus's head, forcing him still as he pressed the cloth again, trying to stem the endless bleed.

"Was Miriana here?" Valcom demanded, his voice tight with fear.

Igneus's laughter tapered into ragged gasps. Slowly, he nodded.

"Oh god," Valcom cursed, voice breaking as he ducked beneath Igneus's arm. He hauled him upward, staggering under the weight. Igneus's body convulsed, and a wet gurgle rose from his throat. A rush of blood spilled from his lips, splattering across the marble floor in a vivid arc.

"Shit," Valcom muttered, his face paling. Igneus's skin was ghostly, slick with sweat, his eyes glassy. He groaned as Valcom slung his arm across his shoulders, propping him against his own body.

"We need to find her," Valcom pressed urgently. "You'll have to walk. Can you do that?"

A weak whimper escaped Igneus. It was all the answer Valcom needed. He tightened his grip, jaw clenched, and together the brothers lurched forward, hobbling through a corridor drowned in darkness. No torchlight reached this place; only their ragged breathing and the dragging shuffle of boots echoed in the silence.

The marble underfoot clicked with each unsteady step, until Igneus froze. Something glimmered faintly. He stooped with a groan, his fingers closing around a decorative orb the size of a large grape—red glass that caught the meager light. He turned it over in his palm, face twisting with some unspoken thought.

Then, with a hiss of pain, he leaned against the wall and forced his eyelid wide.

"Don't—" Valcom started, too late.

Igneus shoved the marble into his ruined socket. His body seized, a ragged groan tearing from his chest. The orb slid into place with a grotesque snugness, his eyelid twitching as he blinked and blinked, seething through clenched teeth until the agony dulled into something almost bearable. His chest rose and fell in shallow, rasping gulps.

Valcom steadied him once more. Igneus swayed, dazed, but still moving. Together they staggered toward the throne room.

***

Miriana stood there in the throne room, ready with her sword drawn, the steel trembling in her grip. Her chest still heaved with the weight of what she had seen, of what she had done.

143

"Miriana!"

Amalia and Neel rushed to her side. Their eyes were bright with concern.

"Are you both—are you safe?" Miriana gasped.

"We're fine," Amalia said quickly, her eyes darting over her friend.

"I left him," Miriana choked suddenly. "My uncle." The words broke from her lips as though she had only just realized them.

"There was nothing you could have done," Neel said quietly, but firmly.

Her knees trembled as they walked, Amalia and Neel clutching her arms just in case. Exhaustion pulled at all three, but Miriana's face was carved with guilt. A man who had raised her, who had given her her first sword, was abandoned.

"He's dead," she whispered, voice cracking. Her lungs rattled with shallow, uneven breaths.

Neel spun, forcing her to face him. "Miriana, your uncle... look, I'm his biggest fan. He's awesome."

Amalia coughed, unimpressed.

"But—" Neel pressed on, ignoring her, "he's alive. Everyone's alive."

Before she could answer, running footsteps thundered behind them.

The king and queen swept into the throne room through the grand entrance, both pale and shaken. They opened their mouths to speak, but Cedric froze, his hand trembling as he pointed toward the throne.

A cloaked figure sat upon it.

The figure rose slowly, deliberately, as though savoring the audience. With one motion, the hood was flung back, and golden hair spilled free in bouncing waves. Emerald eyes glimmered like cut glass, burning with cold intensity. Lips too perfect to be cruelly twisted into a sneer.

"Juliet!" Queen Vivian cried, horror in her voice.

Out of the corner of her eye, Miriana saw Igneus and Valcom stumble into the chamber. Igneus leaned heavily on his brother, one eye hidden, the other bleak with pain. Their gaze met hers. The smallest, saddest smile flickered across his face, an apology in silence. It was all he could give.

Juliet's voice cracked like a whip, commanding all attention. "Do you see me now, Mother? Do you finally see who I am?"

She climbed onto the arms of the throne like a stage, the robe slipping from her shoulders. It fell to the floor, revealing a fitted leather riding suit, dark brown, cinched at the waist with a belt that carried a saber. Her fingers hovered possessively over the hilt.

"Juliet," Cedric's voice thundered, though his body trembled, "what is the meaning of this? Get down at once!"

Their gazes locked , the ferocity of his daughter's look caused him to falter first.

"You don't know," she whispered, her voice dripping with venom. "You don't know what it's like to be shoved aside. To be traded as a bargaining chip for alliances." Her eyes cut to her mother, then her father. "No one is coming. They are dead and it is just us. You have run out of help."

Her saber rang as she unsheathed it, blade gleaming like cold fire. She leveled the point not at her parents, but at Igneus and Valcom.

Miriana's grip tightened on her own hilt, feet braced, heart pounding. Juliet's laugh rang sharp and cruel.

"I paid that man to kill you," Juliet spat. "So the kingdom would hunt him, never suspect me. I am the princess. Who would accuse me? And when the king and queen fell, chaos would reign. I am unwed, untrained—but I would step forward, the isle's savior. I have studied books of strategy, of war, of rule. I learned to fight, to lead. To be a queen."

King Cedric's face blanched and Queen Vivian gagged as if struck.

Juliet's eyes glittered with triumph. "What do you think of my plan, Mother? Father?"

She jumped down from the throne, her boots echoing on the stone, the saber now angled at her parents. Her steps were measured, deliberate.

Miriana slid between them, blade raised, its tip pressing toward Juliet's breast.

"I don't like them either," she growled, "but I'm done with people dying. Back. Off."

"Uh—Miriana?" Neel hissed, teeth clenched. "What are you doing?"

But she did not move. She did not blink.

Then, soft fingers touched her shoulder.

Queen Vivian stepped past her, toward her daughter. Her voice shook with a maternal ache.

"My daughter," she whispered. "I am sorry. Sorry that this is the land you must grow in. Sorry, it is not the one you deserve. We tried to give you everything. Everything you could ever want."

Juliet's saber did not waver. Her eyes burned into Miriana, unyielding.

Vivian reached her, hands trembling as they came to rest gently upon Juliet's shoulders. "Everything," she whispered again, eyes glistening.

Lightning-fast, Juliet thrust, steel punching into flesh.

Queen Vivian gasped as red bloomed across her gown. Her eyes rolled back as she crumpled. Juliet caught her head with one hand, forcing her to look up. Blood spilled from her mouth in gurgling rivulets.

Juliet leaned close, lips brushing her ear.

"Everything," she hissed, "but the crown."

She ripped the blade free. Vivian collapsed, face-first onto the stone. Her blood spread outward in a widening pool.

Juliet's hands dripped red. Her mother's lifeless eyes stared wide, fixed on her daughter with terror and disbelief.

For a heartbeat, the room held its breath. Then something impossible happened. From the wound where Juliet's blade had pierced her mother, a thin plume of blue smoke coiled upward, luminous as a lantern and smelling faintly of a garden. The air around Queen Vivian seemed to cool; her face paled until her eyes took on an inky, glassy blue. The breath left her with a single, small exhalation, and her body sagged, collapsing to the stone with a dead weight.

Juliet stood there, blade slick in her hand, bewilderment flashing across her youth and rage. She staggered back as if the world itself had betrayed her. For a moment, she stared at the corpse, then at the stunned faces filling the hall.

Chaos snapped like a tightened wire. People screamed and surged forward. King Cedric lunged to his wife's side, scooping her up with hands stained ruby.

Her blood spread across his royal robes as he held her like something fragile and impossible. Her eyes stared up at him. Empty and gone.

Juliet's voice was low and hard. "I suppose I wasn't the only one with secrets." She turned, slow and deliberate, to the frozen assembly and approached her father as if walking a stage.

"Have you ever known… that she was a witch?" she asked, the accusation sharp as a dagger.

Cedric merely clutched his wife and rocked, his shoulders shaking with a grief that made him mute. Juliet's frustration curdled into a roar.

"DO YOU SEE ME NOW, FATHER?" she screamed, hair plastered to her face with sweat, eyes raw and wild. Tears tracked silent, hot lines down his cheeks, and he could not meet hers.

"Look at me! See me!" she shrieked, brandishing the saber in a manic arc. Then she charged.

Miriana threw herself forward, blade raised. The two collided in a flash of steel. Juliet's saber glanced inches from Miriana's cheek. Miriana flipped her sword in her hand and drove it toward the princess's flank, scoring a shallow line. Juliet snarled and brought her blade down in a vicious arc aimed at Miriana's skull. Miriana was quicker; she twisted free, flipped away, and with a hard, glancing kick connected with Juliet's face. The princess staggered, fingers flying to her nose that was now drenched with blood.

Juliet lunged again, aimed for Miriana's gut. Miriana pivoted, lifted her knee, and collided with Juliet's chest. The contact turned the assault into a scramble. Miriana elbowed Juliet in the broken bridge of her nose. The princess yelped and dropped her saber.

Miriana wasted no time. She slid a foot under the fallen blade, booting it into the air and catching it behind her back. She then poised the steel at its owner's throat, twin weapons now aligned: Miriana's one hand, Juliet's the other. For a moment, Miriana allowed herself a small, sharp smile.

Juliet's gaze swung to her father, then to her mother, still clutched in his hands. "I hired him to do it," she spat, venom cracking her voice. "So that I might remain the dutiful *daughter*. But he was a coward; he would not act."

"The man who taught me is righteous," she sneered, "strong enough to see greatness and bow to it." She whipped her head toward the doorway, expecting him. Realizing he wouldn't appear at the mention of him, she turned back to the small group. Her face wild and triumphant. "Bow!" she screamed.

The king's stare cut into her for a heartbeat, slow and unreadable. At that precise flicker of distraction, Miriana surged. She launched herself at Juliet, unsheathed and sweeping, and pinned the princess, blade pressing hot to Juliet's throat.

Juliet's lips curled. "You dare defy your queen?" she hissed. In a brutal, spiteful motion, she stomped down on Miriana's toes. Miriana cried out, staggering back. Juliet followed with an elbow to Miriana's throat; Miriana gagged, hacking for air as the world tunneled for a moment.

Igneus lunged to her aid out of Valcom's shoulder, his movements a raw blur. Her friends closed in hot behind him.

"Don't take another step or I'll slit her head from her shoulders!" Juliet screamed, voice cutting the room like a blade. The threat froze everyone in place. Miriana lay clutching her throat, desperate; her own sword skidded just out of reach. Juliet reached down and plucked up her personal blade.

Juliet's face was triumph incarnate. "That's better," she breathed. But the moment stretched, taut and dangerous, then, impossibly, King Cedric moved.

He had slid behind his daughter while the others were distracted. Swiftly, without missing a second, he seized Miriana's fallen sword. With hands shaking, face raw with grief and fury, he plunged it into Juliet's heart.

The hall fell into a void of sound. Juliet's scream chewed the air for a single, terrible instant, and then she slumped, the life leaving her like air from a bellows. Cedric's tears burned hot against the blood on his cheeks; his hands trembled as he let the sword slip from his grasp. He stared at what he had done as if waking from a dream.

"The princess—" Amalia gasped, the words shredded and small.

The group moved, some making to flee, some frozen. Footsteps thundered behind them. Romof and his band swept past the room, hair and leathers glaring, their boots ringing on the stone. As they ran, Romof's voice carried back, cold and triumphant. "I think the kitchen is somewhere up here!" he called.

Igneus kept his head bowed, fury and blood and exhaustion a tight knot in his chest. Valcom tugged at the king, trying to steady him even as Cedric made a futile lunge towards the door after Romof. The words of the mob washed past. "Anarchy," "Sending a message," and other chants that barely brushed the group as the hunters melted away, not even sparing the supposed heroes a glance.

Miriana wrenched free of her friends' hands and tore after the retreating figures. "Miriana!" the twins cried, sprinting to catch her. Her voice was a low, lethal thing. "We're going to make them pay." The words fell like iron; even her friends faltered at the coldness in them.

"I'm going to make them all pay," she promised, legs churning, closing the gap.

"What's the plan?" Amalia panted behind her.

Miriana's jaw set. "Sometimes the best plan… is no plan." She gave a smile that was almost a snarl, twisted her face.

Igneus, supported by Valcom, pushed himself upright and glared after his family. He gathered the last of his strength and hissed, "Let's go stop them with our little hero."

"Romof!" he shouted at his old mentor as members of the Wings of Massacre brought in large burlap sacks and began piling them in their arms. Miriana and the group rounded the corner and stood ready to attack. Igneus hurled a knife with a hard, animal sound. It slid through the air and nicked Romof's cheek, embedding itself in a tapestry at the far end of the hall with a muffled *thud*.

"Boy," Romof spat without turning, "you play with the devil's right hand!" Then he whirled and, with the speed of a predator, turned and flicked a dagger of his own from his belt, launching it at Igneus's chest.

Igneus twisted, the blade grazing past him. He spun, sliding behind Romof and seizing him in a savage clinch—arm around the man's throat, dagger point pressed to the soft flesh beneath Romof's jaw. For a breath, it looked as if the apprentice had the master by the throat.

Romof's reflex was a vicious slash; he cut Igneus's arm and used his leverage to flip him over his shoulder. Igneus crashed down onto the ancient carpet with a heavy thud, dust puffing up from the weave as he landed hard.

Igneus twisted his wrist, jabbing the knife backward. The blade bit deep into Romof's thigh. A crimson stream burst free, staining the carpet as Romof howled. His leg buckled, but he lashed back with a savage kick, his boot colliding with Igneus's head. Igneus toppled sideways with a groan, vision sparking white.

"You were always soft, boy," Romof spat, voice ragged with pain. "Always hesitant." He raised the dagger high and drove it down for Igneus's throat.

Valcom caught his wrist mid-strike. Their arms trembled, veins bulging, as the steel hovered inches from his brother's skin. Desperate, Igneus shoved at Romof's scarred face with his free hand, forcing space, then rammed his knee into Romof's groin. Romof crumpled off him with a strangled groan and in the same movement took Valcom tumbling down with him.

But the reprieve was brief. With a guttural snarl, Romof plunged his dagger into Igneus's side. The steel buried itself to the hilt. Igneus's scream tore through the chamber. Romof twisted the blade. Pain lit Igneus's nerves like wildfire; his teeth ground together as he ripped Romof's arm free and clutched at the wound, blood spilling hot and fast between his fingers. Already, his skin had gone pale as parchment.

While they grappled, Miriana seized the king by the arms. "Come with me, Your Majesty. Quickly now," she urged, her voice taut with urgency.

He hesitated, frozen in disbelief.

King Cedric's gaze locked on her. "But… you were one of the three sentenced to hang," he stammered.

Miriana gave a harsh, humorless laugh. "Yeah, that didn't work out. So, what's it going to be? Lose your head here, or keep it and move?"

His mouth opened, then shut. At last, he nodded and followed.

Outside the chamber, two armored knights lay sprawled across the threshold, their helmets gone, their throats cut open to the bone. Blood pooled beneath them in dark mirrors of their faces. Miriana dragged the royal through the once-grand halls—now wreckage. Portraits hung askew or lay shattered on the floor. The marble echoed with distant screams, bootfalls, and the thundering chaos of the Wings of Massacre. Servants scattered like mice, some crying, some carrying nothing but their own fear.

"The knights have left us," Cedric panted as he stumbled at Miriana's side. His voice was heavy with despair.

Miriana felt the absence too. The halls rang empty but for their footfalls, eerie in their stillness. She craned her head toward Neel and Amalia, who trailed them, breath ragged. "Where are the guards?" she demanded. They only shook their heads, gasping.

Suddenly, Cedric stopped short, face tight with a terrible resolve. "I must go back. My wife." He spun and sprinted for the throne room, ignoring every plea that followed after him.

Valcom's head snapped after him. Igneus groaned, clutching his bleeding side, prying his brother's supporting arm off his shoulders. Propped against the wall, he wheezed, "Get that fool out. I'll manage myself for a while."

"Don't be an idiot," Valcom shot back, but the look in Igneus's single eye hardened, steel beneath pain.

"We're in deep shit either way," he rasped. "Especially me. Go."

Valcom hesitated. Then, with a choked breath, he nodded. "I'll be right back." And he tore down the corridor after the king, ribs screaming with every stride.

He flung open the throne room doors, panting, fire in his lungs. Inside, Cedric knelt, his knees soaking in his wife's blood, clutching her limp body. His sobs filled the vast, hollow chamber.

"It was an arranged marriage," Cedric gasped, his voice raw. Valcom approached slowly, silently.

"We were so young," Cedric choked. "Neither of us wanted it. But when Juliet came... she was our truce. We played the part, lived the lie. And now... now this pain... if it was only an act, why does it devour me?" His howl rattled the rafters.

"Maybe you began to love her," Valcom murmured, standing beside him, eyes fixed forward, not daring to meet the sight of Vivian's body.

Tears streamed unchecked down Cedric's face. "This is my fault."

"No," Valcom said softly. "It's the princess's."

Cedric's head snapped toward him, fury incarnate. "And how do you think she became that way?!" he roared, spittle spraying the air. His bloodshot eyes bulged; his face was scarlet, veins pulsing at his temple. He was rage itself, godlike in his grief.

Valcom dropped his head low. "Forgive me. I spoke out of turn. And about your daughter, no less." He bowed deeply.

Cedric's breathing slowed, his face paling back toward human color. He shifted Vivian gently in his arms, scratching absently at his van dyke. His voice was quieter when he spoke. "You're very respectable… for a marauder who stole into my palace."

Valcom shook his head. "I'm not with them. But they haven't left yet. If we don't escape, the kingdom will drown in chaos."

Cedric stared at his wife's face for a long moment. "I won't leave her."

"Then we'll take her with us," Valcom said simply.

With trembling care, Cedric lifted Vivian into his arms again, bracing his knees to stand. Valcom pressed a hand against his back to steady him.

Together, they turned for the door, only to stop short.

The Wings of Massacre then poured into the throne room like a tide, dragging captives in tow. They placed large bags in the center of the room. At their head strode Romof. He stood before a growing mound of flour sacks piled high, a match poised between his fingers, flame licking dangerously close to the burlap.

Igneus stumbled into view, his hand pressed to his side, his body a husk of will and fury. His voice cracked the air. "What are you doing?"

Romof's scarred face twisted into something like nostalgia. "When I was a boy, I helped my late mother in her kitchen. She was a baker's wife." He rolled the match idly between his fingers, eyes distant. "I saved coins for months to buy her a candle. She would always hum to herself as she worked on her stitching at night. I dropped it once into a cloud of flour. And *fwoom*." He mimed the explosion with relish. "The whole pile went up in fire. My father snuffed it out with an apron. But I… I never forgot the lesson." He began to pace around the packs. "Did you know that flour can be explosive? The carbohydrates in the dust, when on fire, set off a chain reaction."

He stopped and leaned forward over the pile, flame dancing closer to the sacks. "A bakery needs flour to feed a village. But a mountain of flour? A mountain can burn a kingdom. And I've learned to wield that power."

Igneus's voice was hoarse, his body swaying. "You'll kill your own men. Even if we survive, they'll burn with the rest of us."

CHAPTER EIGHT

"All for the good of the cost," Romof growled.

He dropped the match onto the stacked pile as did his followers. Flames sprouted instantly, licking hungrily at the bags until loud popping noises gasped from the spaces within. A thunderous *boom* followed, shaking the air.

Igneus staggered backwards, dazed, his instincts screaming at him to run, though his body refused to obey. The acrid scent of burning starch and fabric clawed at his throat. Then—through the haze—he saw his brother and kin rushing back toward the room, drawn by the strange noises.

"Get out!" Igneus screamed as they approached. Another explosion tore through the chamber, this one violent enough to make the walls tremble. Cedric was thrown into Igneus, who caught him by the arm and half-dragged, half-carried him toward the passage. Valcom stumbled behind, gasping, the heat of the inferno at their backs.

Their niece and friends were waiting at the doorway, wide-eyed. Miriana shrieked, "Valcom, what are you doing?"

Valcom had stopped short in another room, pleading with Romof to leave. "Leave with us, please," he begged, "I don't want any more people to die."

Romof turned, eyes burning with conviction. "Down with the monarchies, up with the people!"

He smiled coldly at Igneus. "You should have stayed dead, son."

The blast that followed devoured the air itself. Dust and smoke surged through the corridors like a living storm. Screams tore the night apart as cracks spidered through the marble floors, racing toward their victims, snaring them in doom's web. Then the world gave way.

The castle collapsed beneath its own grandeur. Rubble poured like rain from high walls; ancient stones split open with deep, mournful groans. The survivors stumbled through the corridor, coughing, eyes stinging, as the once-mighty fortress became a tomb of smoke and ruin.

Smoke clogged their lungs as they crawled from the wreckage. Neel brushed dust off himself as he went over to help the crawling Amalia up. Miriana blinked furiously to clear her eyes, the world reduced to gray ash and broken light. Through her blurred vision, she spotted a limping figure — a member of the Massacre, trying to escape.

She staggered after him, wrenching a jagged shard of rebar from the debris. When Romof turned, he saw her only for an instant before she drove the metal through him.

He fell with a hoarse moan, stirring the dust once more. His eyes dulled, his fingers twitched once, twice, then went still as his soul slipped away.

Miriana gasped, a sob tearing from her throat as she collapsed to her knees. She knelt amid the ruin, shaking, breath ragged with grief. Behind her, the crunch of shifting debris announced Neel and Amalia's arrival. They knelt beside her, silent, each trapped in their own storm of thought.

"Oh, god!" a voice bellowed. It was raw and desperate. The echo ricocheted through the broken halls.

"Igneus?" Miriana breathed. She sprang up, heart pounding, and sprinted back toward the mountain of collapsed stone.

"Igneus?" she shouted, her voice rebounding through the emptiness. "Uncle?"

A great stone tumbled from above. Miriana climbed, slipping, skin tearing on sharp edges as she clawed her way upward. Her friends followed, hands raw and bleeding, shoving aside shattered stone. When the rubble shifted, they froze—there was fabric, soaked in red.

A hand burst through the cracks, trembling, reaching for air. The group seized it, pulling desperately until a man emerged from the wreckage — bloodied, his chainmail splintered, crimson life streaking his face and chest. His single good eye widened in disbelief. Amalia clapped a hand to her mouth. Neel went pale. Miriana, his niece, could only gape wordlessly. They all finally could spare a few seconds to study what had happened to the man.

"They took my eye," Igneus rasped.

Miriana nodded. "I noticed," she murmured, dragging him free from the ruin. He was a ruin himself — bruised, dust-caked, his arm hanging useless at his side.

"I think you broke your arm," Miriana said gently. Igneus looked down and winced.

"I noticed," he muttered.

"I thought you died."

"Well, that's a horrible insult," he smiled.

"I last saw Valcom in the throne room," Igneus said suddenly, breaking the silence. He tried to walk without limping, though every step betrayed him. Miriana's gaze fell to his leg with pity, but whenever she tried to meet his eye, he turned away.

He groaned, stooping lower under invisible weight. Miriana placed a steadying hand on his back, while Neel and Amalia crouched to meet his gaze.

"You're amazing, sir, true, but if you need to take a rest…?" Neel ventured.

"*I don't need rest; we need to find Valcom!*" Igneus thundered. Neel recoiled awkwardly while Amalia made a small noise of distaste.

Silence fell again. Neel shot Amalia an I told you *so* look; she elbowed him lightly, and together they began to climb down from the mountain of wreckage, leaving uncle and niece in the trembling light of dawn.

"Banged up?" Igneus asked.

"Been through worse," Miriana responded.

The faint crackle of dying fire echoed around them. Smoke drifted in lazy coils above the rubble where stone and steel lay melted together. Miriana turned toward the edge of the ruin, where a body lay half-buried — Romof's, the twisted steel still jutting grotesquely from his back. Igneus followed her gaze, his expression unreadable.

"You killed him."

Miriana didn't answer. She turned away, shoulders stiff, face shadowed by ash and remorse.

"Only I was allowed to do that," Igneus said quietly. "You… shouldn't have done that. It was my revenge."

"I stopped the villain!" Miriana spat.

Igneus shifted, wincing, bracing himself on one good arm as gravel slid beneath him. He met her eyes with his one remaining eye — a tired, dark ember of judgment and grief.

"It was my problem. I would've handled it," he explained.

Miriana scoffed, her voice raw. "You made him all of our problems the moment you took the job. Plus, you could have quit the Massacre way before this! Why would you think 'oh we're in a struggling family. We need extra money. I'll just be an assassin?!'"

"I was young and stupid."

"Yes, that much is obvious."

"But I own that, I'm making up for it."

"Making up for it?" Miriana spat back, the word sharp as a blade.

Igneus flinched. "I'm working on — I-I didn't have a good—"

"So, you are going to give other people bad childhoods and lives to make up for the fact that yours was horrid?"

Igneus opened and closed his mouth like a fish, searching for words that refused to come.

Miriana rose slowly. In that moment, silhouetted against the smoke and ruin, she looked every bit the woman he had hoped she would become — strong, unyielding, and furious.

"You are too late to fix anything, uncle," she seethed.

She grasped his good arm and hauled him to a clumsy stand. Together they stumbled down toward the twins, the silence between them thick as ash. Neither looked the other in the eye.

"Where did you say you saw Valcom?" she asked.

"He went back for the king," Igneus responded icily.

"I got the king out of the throne room already," Miriana said.

They exchanged uneasy glances, searching for a way out through the fractured underbelly of the castle.

"He went back for his wife's body," Igneus murmured after a moment. "Valcom went after him at the time of the explosions."

A flicker of light caught Amalia's eye on the north wall — faint, quivering. "There," she breathed, pointing. They hurried toward the glimmer, hearts pounding. Igneus crouched as low as his broken body would allow, inspecting the crack that shimmered faintly in the gloom.

"The wall is weak," he said, "If we ram it, it should give way for us to escape." Neel smiled as he ran as far back as the rubble would allow. Leading with his shoulder, Neel ran as fast as he could into the crumbling wall. Stones tumbled down and new cracks formed, stretching across the face.

Miriana and Amalia walked over and stood on both sides of him.

"Let's try one more time," Miriana suggested. Neel smiled at her warmly. The three of them charged at the surface then. A thunderous crash rang in their ears as plumes of dust were kicked up.

They all waved the soot away from their faces as the fallen barricade came into view, light flooding into the cavern.

"Jericho has fallen." Igneus laughed as the group headed into the passage.

The once resplendent marble was now chipped with cracks spiderwebbing across the surface. Artworks, mirrors, and windows were destroyed with glass littering the broken floorways. Amalia tiptoed around the shards. Suits of armor were crushed under the weight of large debris.

They rounded the corner when Miriana shouted in surprise. At the end of the corridor squatted a man with unruly hair. His eyes were red and wet with grief. He crouched nearby with his grimy hands clutching his head. His crown and cape were gone; in the flickering torchlight, he looked like any other broken man. *She supposed he was now,* Miriana thought. The king. In front of him, in a makeshift grave covered by a tapestry, the queen.

Neel went over to him and knelt down to his level, "Your Highness, we need to leave." He gently grabs King Cedric's arm and wraps it around his shoulder, lifting him up.

"Not yet."

Leaning against the destroyed wall was Igneus, his face gray with pain, one hand clutching his side.

"We need to find Valcom," he huffed.

"We're going to. Where did we last see him? In the castle? Where do we start looking?" Miriana cried.

"He fell through the ground," Cedric said, his voice ragged but concerningly steady, "He's somewhere further down. Based on where I think he was standing in the throne room, I think I know exactly where he is. We can get there this way." The king leaned against Neel as he pointed down the path.

In the deep cavern of the fortress, smoke and dust billowed thickly through the ruined chamber, swallowing the air. Valcom wiped at his eyes, tears mixing with grit as he struggled to see. The floor above him had collapsed — a jagged wound in the ceiling through which he had fallen. Marble slabs and shattered stone surrounded him, stacked high like the walls of a tomb, sealing off the hole above.

He staggered upright, tugging at his cloak, which was snagged on a piece of broken rebar. His knees trembled, his chest ached, and his breathing came shallow and quick. When his vision cleared, he realized where he had landed — a buried library.

Bookshelves climbed the walls from floor to ceiling, their spines glinting faintly like jewels beneath a layer of soot. Leather bindings of every color — deep reds, sea greens, the faded blues of forgotten ages — caught the flicker of light as the iron torches along the walls suddenly flared to life. The flames threw long, trembling shadows across the room, transforming the dust into drifting ghosts.

Valcom coughed hard, the sound rasping in the silence. His lungs burned with smoke and despair. Then, faintly, beneath the echo of his own hacking, came a sound.

"Valcom," a voice sang — soft and melodic — echoing through the cavernous space. The name multiplied in the ruin, as though a choir of unseen throats whispered it back to him.

"Who's there?! Show yourself!" his hoarse voice cracked. He coughed again, spitting dust, scanning the shifting gloom.

But there was no reply. Only the steady crumble of loose debris and his own ragged breathing filled the air.

"Come now! "Come now! I am in no mood for games," Valcom muttered, wiping his brow and smearing dirt and blood into a streaked mask. He limped deeper into the library, hand pressed against his bruised ribs, eyes darting from shadow to shadow.

"*Valcom,*" the voice crooned again.

"*Please,*" Valcom begged, the strength in his voice faltering. "My family is missing. Or hurt. If you know where I am or a way out… I would be endlessly grateful."

Silence fell again — heavy, almost reverent. He let out a low growl of frustration and moved forward, his boots crunching on fallen plaster. Towering marble columns loomed on either side of him, their cracked surfaces carved with faces that seemed to shift in the wavering torchlight. Their shadows twisted across the floor like restless spirits.

A soft *thwip* — the sound of a page turning — echoed behind him. Valcom spun on his heel, heart pounding.

There, in the center of the room, stood a solitary desk and chair. The desk gleamed faintly, impossibly polished amid the ruin. Its candle had long since burnt to nothing but a stub of wax. The chair was cushioned with satin pillows — untouched by dust, as though waiting for its master to return.

Upon the desk lay a small book bound in purple leather. Its cover shimmered faintly when he approached, and its pages, though yellowed with age, still bore ink as black and vivid as if just used.

Valcom reached out, his fingers trembling, still clutching his aching side with his other hand. The book quivered under his touch — almost alive.

"*Valcom*," the voice whispered again, this time from beneath him.

His breath caught. "No… that's not… no sense…" he muttered, bending to lift the book. He opened it carefully. The pages were filled with a strange, flowing script — no tongue he recognized, the letters looping like vines. He mouthed them, curious, his lips shaping nonsense.

Valcom gave a dry laugh. The words sounded absurd.

"Illian saem eth draven vesp."

The instant the words left his mouth, the air shifted — sharp, unnatural. A freezing pain erupted in his gut and raced outward through his veins. He staggered backward with a cry, the book slipping from his hands and hitting the marble floor without a sound.

The cold spread like fire in reverse — seizing his chest, his limbs, his skull. Frost bloomed along his fingertips, glistening pale blue. His breath turned to mist before him, hanging in the air like a spirit before fading away.

Then, as suddenly as it had begun, the chill vanished. Warmth flooded back into his body.

Valcom stood trembling, sweat beading his forehead. He shuddered violently, trying to shake off the haunting sensation. Then, with hesitant curiosity, he bent and retrieved the fallen book.

He stared at his hands. The cuts and bruises were gone. Tentatively, he touched his temple — the gash, the dried blood, all vanished. His breath hitched. *I'm healed,* he realized. *Whole.*

A laugh escaped him — incredulous at first, then wild. He jumped once, twice, as though testing his restored strength. "*I feel… healthy,*" he murmured, almost in awe. Then another laugh bubbled out — and another.

Soon he was dancing across the library, the purple book clutched to his chest, spinning among the drifting dust. Giggles and cackles echoed off the shelves until the sound grew strange — too bright, too sharp.

Smiling like a church boy, he opens the book again and begins to browse the pages.

"Valcom!"

He froze. The voice was different now — real. He turned to see his companions climbing through a jagged hole in the wall, coughing as dust cascaded from above.

"We need to get out of here. Now," Neel said urgently.

"Cedric, how do we get out of here?" Miriana demanded, turning to .

She glanced toward Igneus — her uncle's gaze met hers, one eye blue and the other a deep, unnatural red.

The king pushed himself unsteadily away from Neel and placed a trembling hand on Igneus's shoulder. "There is a hidden passage. In the hallway. You set a little portrait on the corner of this little table — it opens it."

"Oh," Neel exclaimed, rummaging through his shirt. "I know where that is. I haven't had the time to sell the gold frame yet." He pulled out a small portrait frame, now grimy but intact.

"Well, we have the key," Valcom said, his voice airy and strange. He strode toward the shattered doorway, the purple book still warm in his grasp. "Let's go find the table."

He waved them onward with a smile that didn't quite reach his eyes.

"We will be safe once we reach my tavern," Valcom comforted.

Igneus leaned heavily on his brother's shoulder, using him as a crutch. The twins followed close behind, their faces streaked with soot and fear. Miriana lingered near the king, who had collapsed against a cracked pillar, his royal finery torn to rags. She reached for his arm, steadying him.

"We need to go," she whispered.

The king nodded weakly and stumbled forward as the group moved down the ruined corridor. Their footsteps echoed in hollow rhythm, chased by the trembling of the castle's dying foundations.

"Over here!" Neel shouted, sprinting ahead. They rounded the corner after him, the air thick with dust and the groan of shifting stone. The walls had cracks and holes. Portraits were ripped and the smell of smoke lingered in the air.

"Here," he called, setting the golden frame upright on the corner of a narrow table as the rest caught up.

They waited.

"Nothing happened," Amalia pouted, wiping at her brow.

The castle shuddered violently as the wreckage was settling. Valcom reached out, catching both his brother and the king before they could fall. They didn't have much time.

"Do I have to push it?" Neel wondered aloud. He pressed down on the frame. The corner sank with a low *click*, followed by the sound of gears grinding somewhere deep beneath them.

A moment later, the tiles beneath their feet trembled, then slowly descended. Dust rose around them as the floor lowered and became a landing. The darkness revealed a dark, narrow stairway.

They exchanged wary glances but said nothing as they sank into the shadows.

The passage below smelled of damp stone and iron. The walls were slick, carved centuries ago, lined with trickles of water that glimmered in the faint torchlight. Every step echoed off unseen corners.

"Why would you need this?" Valcom asked softly, clutching the purple book close to his chest as if it could protect him.

The king frowned, voice rasping. "So," he choked, "so if something like this happened, we could escape."

They pressed onward until a rusted grate appeared ahead. The twins and Miriana heaved it aside, the metal screeching, and pale daylight spilled through the opening. One by one, they climbed into the open air — freedom, at last.

From there, the group made their way through backstreets and smoke-stained alleys until the familiar sign of Valcom's tavern loomed ahead, its shutters closed, its wood splintering by time and weather.

Cedric's voice broke through their brief calm. "So, this is it?" he asked, glancing around the tavern.

The shutters of the tavern creaked in the wind, letting in long beams of orange dusk. The breeze moaned through the loose boards, whispering through the quiet like a warning. Five horses stood tethered to the posts, shifting uneasily and tugging at their reins.

"I'll get them," Amalia muttered, jogging out the door. "Cruel drunkards," she grumbled under her breath, untying the horses one by one. The horses trotted away from the people to go graze on the nearby meadow.

***

When inside, the air was cooler, the silence thick. Valcom disappeared into his small back room when he entered, while Igneus leaned against the counter, struggling to stay upright.

In his space, Valcom collapsed onto the thin, rigid cot that served as his bed. The room was sparse — one cracked window, a rickety chair, a single shelf lined with dusty bottles. A faint breeze seeped through the wooden wall, rustling his blond hair. He lay back, one foot propped over his knee, tapping idly to the rhythm of his still-racing heart.

His once-white shirt clung to him, browned with sweat and dirt, but he scarcely cared. His focus was on the small purple leather book in his hands. It had become his solace, his secret. When the world felt empty, it seemed to murmur to him — soft words of affection and comfort that no one else ever offered.

To him, it became more than a relic; it was a companion.

He mouthed the strange words as he read, smiling faintly. He stayed on his cot for hours as his friends and family helped themselves to his wares, freely. He scarcely could care. Igneus, though, grew suspicious as the hours waned on. He determinedly then hobbled back to the apartments as the others sat themselves at the tables.

"What is the book even about?" his brother asked, entering without knocking. He poked at the cover, breaking Valcom's trance. The interruption came just as the text had taken an intriguing turn.

"It's a linguistic book. I'm learning a new language. I found it at the castle and was drawn to it," Valcom said evenly, though his smile tightened.

Igneus sat on the edge of the cot, forcing Valcom to draw his legs back. "What language?" he pressed, leaning closer, trying to catch his brother's eyes.

Valcom creased the corner of a page, then snapped the book shut. He stood abruptly, clutching it to his chest. "What's wrong?" Igneus asked.

"Nothing. I'm going to check on the others," Valcom muttered, his voice clipped.

Igneus rose quickly, limping to get in front of him to block the door. For a long, tense moment, they faced each other — two halves of the same storm. Lightning seemed to crackle in the air between them, silent but palpable.

"You have been harboring that book ever since you found it," Igneus said.

Valcom scoffed. "Just because none of you asked to read it does not mean I'm harboring it. This *book* did not cast our lives into disorder."

At that, Igneus's composure cracked. He clenched his jaw and hardened his eyes at his brother.

"You don't get to judge me when you have been fondling and talking to that book while ignoring our niece. She almost died today," he barked over his shoulder.

Valcom froze. The point hit like a slap.

"It's not the same."

"Our family needs us!" Igneus shouted. "We needed money! I didn't know what to do! I trusted the first kind face who would listen to me. But I don't trust you with that book. You keep it so guarded—you're even stroking it right now!"

Valcom blinked down. His thumb was indeed tracing the spine of the book, tenderly. A soft, distant smile crossed his face.

"It's not the same," he whispered. "This book helps me. You went around killing people you were told were bad. People do bad things sometimes when they feel trapped in a corner."

He met his brother's gaze, that one fierce blue eye burning with restrained fury.

"How much different is that from what you were doing, brother?"

Valcom brushed past him and walked out, silent, leaving Igneus standing in the stillness of the small room.

Frustration surged through Igneus. He threw the chair backward, the legs scraping harshly against the wooden floor. He almost tripped from the effort, and then turned to follow after his brother, his boots heavy with anger.

But he stopped short at the doorway.

A cloaked figure stood near the bar, speaking in hushed tones to Valcom. The lamplight barely touched the stranger's face. Valcom held his book close to his chest, his posture wary but somehow calm.

Igneus saw him glance sideways, their eyes meeting for the briefest instant — a flicker of disappointment, almost pity. Then Valcom gestured subtly toward where his brother stood. *Yet another cloaked phantom,* Igneus thought. The person turned their hooded head slightly before quickly running out of the tavern. No one else seemed to notice the strange meeting.

"Who was—"

"Do you want to read it? Is that it? Did you want to have it comfort you too? Or did you just want it to cause me pain? Just to take it away from me?!?"

The rest of the party turned to look at the exhausted tavern master. Miriana gingerly stood up and made her way to her uncle.

"We're all stressed. When the panic has quelled, we'll think of a plan," she reassured.

Valcom faced her, his face quickly drained of color. His breathing quickened, and for a fleeting moment, his eyes—sharp and slitted—reflected like those of an adder: green, venomous, unnatural. He quickly turned his violent eyes back to his brother.

Igneus stiffened. "No, brother, I don't. You just seem so…"

Valcom blinked. The serpentine glint faded; his face softened, color returning like water seeping back into stone.

"…Infested," Igneus finished quietly.

Valcom sighed. He placed a hand on his brother's shoulder, a weary smile tugging at his lips. "You worry too much," he chuckled softly, then turned and walked out, the purple book pressed tight to his chest.

Igneus stood there for a long time, staring at the empty doorway. A heaviness coiled in his gut, pulling down what little peace that remained after the night's events.

"Where are you going?" he called.

Valcom murmured something inaudible, still clutching the book close, like a father protecting a frail child.

"I'm going on a walk. Don't wait for me," he said finally, glancing back with a faint smirk and raised brow.

He left the tavern and stepped into the fading daylight. The grass outside swayed with the wind as he wandered down the slope toward the village. His lips moved in quiet conversation—though there was no one beside him.

"You would protect me? Really? Thank you," he whispered, his voice trembling with delight.

Villagers turned as he passed, whispering, uneasy. They went to climb through the remains of the castle for life and treasure. They muttered that they would visit his tavern with accusations of his strange family having a vulgar plot against the isle. Valcom paid them no mind. His eyes gleamed with feverish conviction, as though he were listening to someone—or something—that only he could hear.

"No. No one helped us, none of them," he said bitterly to the empty air. "It's not like the bruises were imaginary. When we would cut wood or receive flour, people would notice and turn their noses."

He laughed softly, shaking his head, his blond hair whipping in the sea wind. The path led him up the cliffs that overlooked the churning ocean below.

"Yes. The people need…" Valcom smiled faintly as he neared the edge.

"The sea," he whispered.

He stood tall on the cliffside, the waves crashing beneath him, salt stinging his face. The wind howled like a living thing, and in it he heard the book's voice again, soft, coaxing, insistent. He flipped through it with reverence. The pages shimmered faintly, casting a dim violet glow.

The whisper grew clearer, beckoning him to repeat.

"Mik'e je igmiuth!" he roared, the words tearing from his throat like a curse. His voice carried on the wind, echoing out to the horizon.

The ocean answered.

It began to boil—first in gentle ripples, then violently, as bubbles the size of shields rose and burst. Fish floated belly-up, eyes white and mouths frozen in silent screams. The water frothed into a sickly white-green foam, a rancid and overwhelming stench rising with it, like the decay of the dead left too long in the sun.

Villagers along the coast screamed. They ran to the shore, clutching their children, watching in horror as their once-blue waters turned to a rotting bog.

Valcom turned to face them, his expression eerily serene. Then he smiled—a wide, proud, triumphant smile—and threw his arms open.

"This," he seemed to declare without words, "is what you made. This is the recompence for your inaction!"

With that, he crouched low and leapt into the air, vanishing into the graying clouds as smoke trailed behind him like ink dissolving in water.

The sky blackened. Thunder cracked the heavens apart. Lightning spidered through the clouds in jagged arcs.

Back at the tavern, the windows rattled with every peal.

The king turned from the storm outside and looked toward the others gathered inside, their faces tired, haunted.

"Still no sign of Valcom," Neel muttered, leaning against the frame, his voice flat with worry.

"How's your mother?" Miriana asked softly.

"Weak, but speaking with enthusiasm," Amalia sighed. "She's been fevered for days. It came on suddenly—one afternoon she was in the garden, the next she could barely stand."

Her brother nodded. "That's why we need the money, you know? For medicine."

Elanor, the twins' mother, lay in a small cottage at the village edge, wrapped in a patchwork of old blankets, shivering as if the chill had lodged in her bones. The sickness had sapped her strength; her skin had turned pale as candlewax. They worried it was a plague or some other terror.

"She's sick?" Igneus breathed, concern threading his voice.

Cedric moved ahead, his shoulders heavy with silence.

"Yes," Amalia said, tilting her head. "She's been sick for a while now. Miriana visits from time to time. You should go. She talks about you."

Neel looked up, his face brightening. "You should visit! You could be even more like an uncle to us!" he squealed, glancing between Igneus and his sister.

"I don't know. I knew Elanor," Igneus said after a long pause. His tone hardened, and he stepped ahead to distance himself from their hopeful faces. "We had a large falling out."

Amalia blinked. "How did you know her?"

"I asked her to be my wife," Igneus said simply.

Neel gasped, nearly tripping over himself. "What?" he cried, his hands clenched beneath his chin in boyish disbelief.

"Your father beat me to it," Igneus murmured. "She was married, and after the wedding, she was busy with her own life."

He didn't look back as he said it. His voice carried the weight of something long buried—and something still bleeding.

"Have I never mentioned this before?" Igneus asked as he tottered past Neel, tilting his head toward the ceiling.

Neel shook his head rapidly, his face flushing pink from holding his breath in anticipation.

"Well," Igneus continued dryly, "that might be because I don't like talking about it."

Neel shrank back, eyes wide, while Miriana stifled a laugh at her friend's expense.

"How sick is she?" Igneus asked, his tone softening.

Amalia folded her arms. "She doesn't leave her bed much anymore. Of course, she's the one cheering us up," she said with a weary smile. "Pa keeps fluffing everything."

Igneus gave a deep chuckle. "How is Paratus?"

"Worried," Amalia replied. "Always about everything." She smirked faintly.

From near the window, Miriana suddenly shouted, "Neel, put the roach down!"

"It's just a spider!"

"That's even worse!" she yelped.

Igneus laughed, the sound low and gravelly. "It's been a long time," he said, still smiling. "I might have to visit."

Amalia stood and walked over, laying a gentle hand on his arm. He arched a brow.

"I know she'd appreciate that," she said warmly. "She might be getting tired of only ever seeing her family's faces."

Neel snorted, and Amalia shot him a sharp look.

Igneus chuckled again, shaking his head. "Never," he teased.

The tavern fell heavy with silence—an uneasy pause between breaths.

Then, the air grew hot.

Igneus looked out the window at the sky, brow furrowed. The temperature spiked again, blistering. The wooden walls began to creak and glow—a deep, unnatural red pulsing beneath the grain.

"Do you feel that?" Neel asked, his voice tight.

The walls shuddered. Then—

Boom!

Flames erupted, swallowing the room in an instant. Heat roared around them; the timbers screamed. Fire licked at the alcohol as if it were begging for parchment. The heat caused the wood to warp and moan in pain as it turned black.

"The Black Book," Cedric whispered, horror catching in his throat.

"Everyone out!" Neel shouted.

They burst through the door just as the tavern exploded into a tower of fire. The inferno climbed toward the night sky, painting the village in shades of gold and blood. The roof collapsed with a deafening crash, sending up a storm of embers that fell like black snow.

And in the heart of the flames—beneath the crackle and roar—came a sound.

A laugh.

Faint at first, then swelling, echoing, curling through the smoke like a living thing.

Valcom's laugh.

CHAPTER NINE

Hours had passed as the party stared at the building. Golden embers still smoldered with a crackle as the heavy taste of smoke still lingered in the air. The group all stood some feet back in disbelief as Igneus approached. The tavern, the *home,* they held dear was destroyed.

"You know, I always found it odd that he wanted to stay," Neel approaches him from behind.

"Maybe because it was the only thing he had ever known." The flickering of embers caused sparks to catch what's left of the lumber into flames. The tavern was like a beacon in the night. Igneus walked further into the flames, his footsteps firm and cautious, and bent down to grab a board to use as a torch in the dark of the night. Without looking behind him, Igneus said, "Everyone, grab the timber. We're going to storm the castle. Again."

"The Black Book," the king inquired urgently, turning to Miriana, "that's what he's been reading?" Miriana looked at him with her eyebrows raised and her lips a tad pursed.

"It was found in your secret library. Wouldn't you know? Are you the author?"

The king sighed. He thudded to the ground. His eyes quickly darted to his ring on his finger, and a heavy sigh escaped his lips. "Long ago," the king began, "I was the son of a smith. I had nothing and seldom did as I was told. I was not allowed near the cliffs, but like the stupid boy I was, I couldn't stop myself." The king paused to take a quivering breath. He looked up at the sky as if he could see his past playing out in front of him.

"I climbed up the stony cliff, and when my toes were right at the edge of it, I leaned my body far over, trying to make out the bottom of the sea. Then a melodious voice came from behind, which shocked me out of my skin. I almost lost my balance and my life that day. 'My, aren't you a young one!' I turned to see a slender woman in a pure white gown with silver trimmings. Her dark hair seemed almost like a dark shade of green, shining like an emerald in a dark mine. I stood there with my mouth agape like a fish. The maiden looked at me with amusing eyes. Then she laughed, and it sounded like a wind chime ringing a tune in my ears. 'I realize that I startled you, child, and for that I apologize. My name is Funus.'

'Funus,' I repeated in a whisper, the sound of it setting a tingle across my tongue, like the taste of pure sugar. It was as if I spoke her name too loud, she would disappear.

'And you? she asked. The amusement in her eyes turned to curiosity.

'Cedric,' I answered begrudgingly as I kicked a clump of grass. She gave another holy laugh.

'But why do you say it like that? That is such a kingly name.' Then it was my turn to laugh. I kicked the turf harder and tipped my head back.

'Lady, no king am I. I'm the son of a smith. I can't read or understand politics. It is far from a kingly name.'

The woman's face went grave, 'Little master,' she uttered. 'Do not joke about the things I tell you. I have seen them. I know you already. When you come to power, my power will cease and my dust will mingle with the shore's sands. I will at last be free from this world. I have seen this.'

I took a step away from the maid, back towards the cliff. My foot gave way, and I sent pebbles skittering down the side. She gave a laugh.

'Worry not, child,' she smiled, her teeth straight and flat, like bovine and as white as their milk.

'I know the future. I have seen your life,' she took a step towards me. I had no place to go. I knew if I stepped back even an inch further, I would meet my demise. So, I stayed rooted.

'How is it you know this?' I quivered. Then she, with her sand-colored hand, reached into her bosom and, with great care, produced a standard book bound with blackberry colored leather. 'The Black Book,' she breathed. At the time, I found it odd how guarded she kept the manuscript. Her fingers were tight around it, guarding it strongly, as if she was afraid that she would commit blasphemy if it fell.

I'm older now. I realize the manuscript would be safe, as long as she is.

She kept the book near her heart, so the only way one may steal it is to kill her. You can become obsessively paranoid as I did when I built that room. She held it out so far in front of her as if admiring pure, shiny gold.

'As per the laws, I cannot tell you exactly what I saw regarding you, but I am always arrogant enough to boast my…heirloom,' she sighed. She minimized the distance between me and her. When she was closer, she opened the yellow pages. Oddly, the words appeared like they were freshly inked.

'The Black Book continues to be the paramount of all our knowledge. Past, present, and its future,' she took another step towards me, more eager. 'And your future begins with meeting me.'

'What power could that have?' I asked her, my breath was shallow, and my eyes only focused on the book's yellow pages.

Suddenly, Funus grabbed me by the lobe of my ear and yanked me towards her face, making me almost fall forward, and hissed, 'Child,' she thrusted the book into my shaking hands, 'do not test me. Men have killed for this knowledge. For this power. And you dare mock the kind maid who gives it to you willingly?"

Wrath shot through her almost purple eyes. The wind seemed to have picked up and a chill went up my spine. The chill reached up and bit at my young neck like a blade holding me hostage unless I accepted the ransom, the Black Book. Though seconds had passed, it seemed like ages, and winter's sleeves began to glitter on my raised arm hair. The cold burned my skin. I hugged the Book closer to my chest, and I felt as if I thawed. Heat seemed to thrum from the Book, spreading its safety and blanket around me, comforting me. Funus smiled at me.

Funus released me from her grasp and spoke with authority, 'I know you'll do great things, Cedric. But be warned, though. You must use the power of this text, so says Time; there is a cost, as there is with everything on Earth. Be it physical or mental, it will be your pride or well-being, bid it come soon or far into the future, be it to empower or affect you. You have to use keen sight. Pay attention.'

I looked down at the Black Book still clutched in my arms. The cold had gone and left me safe and warm. I then look up at my newfound friend.

'What did it cost you if you had used it?' I asked.

She cast her eyes downward, avoiding my questioning gaze. "My only child," she muttered. She looked at me as if she had woken up. As if she were lost somewhere, to the time with her child.

"But that comes later,' she whispered, shaking her head, 'The power feeds off of emotion. There are many of us who are lost or have lost something of ours. Look for her in the future.'

'Who? Your daughter?'

Funus made a grimace at me before a squall of fallen leaves started encircling her, cutting at my eyes. She did not answer my question as her feet lifted off the ground.

'But where does the power come from?' I asked. Funus gave a chuckle that sounded like waves slithering across the beaches and echoing off the cliffs.

'There are many unanswered questions in the universe, boy. Many different theories,' the wind whooshed, and leaves now tornadoed around her more violently. I could barely hear as she said, "I choose to believe it is an entity made when stars die, something bright and pure. Warm; life-giving. Wonder-giving. Something that is too innocent to end. Like the extinction of unicorns, it can only spout dark boons and chaos power. Don't you think so?' I just gawked at her, blanching.

'Use wisely,' she gave a dark smile, then the warm gust of wind completely enveloped her. The squall of leaves and plants seemed to climb over her completely, picking up dirt and stones, trying to take her into the dirt, whilst simultaneously lifting her higher into the air. I couldn't hear or speak as I saw her hands rising, as if summoning someone from the skies. My eyes stung from staring up at the whirling tornado. I think I screamed, but I couldn't hear myself over the roar of the air. When my view was clear and the squall had settled, Funus was gone.

I looked down at the already weighty book, which now felt like it weighed pounds. My hands almost shivered, and I was too scared as I opened the cover. The pages were musty, but the ink was curiously pure and clear, unsmudged writing. I softly began to read the funny-sounding language to myself, not noticing the sudden shift in the air around me."

The party stared at him in complete shock. Neel nursed from his flask. Igneus allowed Neel to have his after the events. Amalia swooned, leaning against a tree for support, her eyes barely open and her chest heaving up and down in slow breaths. Miriana began cleaning her sword, blanching. Igneus squinted at the old king, adjusting to his only seeing eye. He forced himself to be well despite his sight and limp.

"The fire was him?" Amalia whimpered from the spot where she lay almost lifeless.

"Most likely," Cedric answered, "Didn't you hear the laughter?"

Miriana jumped up, sheathing her sword, and went to support her uncle as he teetered on his weak legs. Igneus nodded his thanks and Miriana helped him sit on the grass, his back to his burning home.

"We could round up an army. We'd need to find soldiers," Cedric suggested.

Miriana drove her sword down into its decrepit sheath and marched up to him. Her eyes almost burned him down with a single stare, and she jabbed a finger into his chest.

"We are not going to war against Valcom." She stated each word firmly as if that was her final verdict.

"He's destroying the island. Look what he did here," the king protested.

"Do you think trying to bring him down like this will make it better?!" Miriana's silent threats turned into screams.

Fire sprang up behind the silhouette of the trees. The party turned and watched the gray ashes rise. The ashes reminded Igneus of a blizzard. One from years ago. He shook the thought away.

"Gather the people, Cedric. We march on the castle," Igneus' commanding voice rang through the burning tavern. He was back, and his eyes said that he had made up his mind.

"Finally coming to his senses," King Cedric folded his arms in smug satisfaction. The victory, though, didn't reach his eyes.

"He's your brother," Miriana fumbled and huffed as she staggered up to Igneus. King Cedric quietly left the clearing to gather forces. Neel and Amalia reclined in the grass, carefully watching.

"Cedric has a point," Igneus stated, not looking in Miriana's direction.

"He's always tried to help you!" Now it was Miriana's turn to protest.

"This is the time to put your feelings away," Igneus hissed, turning to her.

"He was there when my parents, your friend and brother, abandoned us." Tears gathered in Miriana's eyes, and her voice went weak and low as she continued her objection.

"Miriana…" Igneus warned.

"He was there when your parents hurt you and finally died," she continued as she stepped towards him.

Igneus grabbed her by the shoulders.

"You really think I want to ki–" he stopped mid-sentence and corrected himself, "fight my brother? He's destroying the island. He razed the ships and boats. There's now no escape," Igneus pointed up the mountain behind him.

"That," he whispered, "is not my brother. That's not your uncle." A singular tear carved a trail down his cheek out of his one good eye. He let go of her shoulders and stepped back in defeat.

Understanding and concern flashed across Miriana's eyes, and she sighed in defeat, raising her eyes to him. She asked, "What do you need?"

"We're going to need horses." Igneus smiles as him and the rest of the company turn to the four creatures Amalia freed, trying to find their way into the forest.

***

A large army loyal to the king filtered into the courtyard. King Cedric had marched through the alleys, imploring for help. Many of his subjects followed after him.

The roar of their anger echoed loudly in Valcom's ears. It sounded familiar — like a fire crackling, but not the tavern he had set ablaze. *More like a memory*, he thought.

The man threw the axe into his son's hands, who fell to the ground with a thump, struggling under its weight. The father scoffed.

"How are you going to be a man if you don't have any strength?"

"But I'm only five."

"Puh. I am not gonna accept that pitiful excuse. Simon was able to cut the logs quickly. He never kept me waiting. And he's only two years older than you." His father scoffed at him.

A tall and strong boy stood off to the side of their father. There was an uncanny resemblance between the two, with dark brown shaggy hair, different from his brother's white. Freckles sprinkled across their noses, compared to Valcom's pale, milky complexion. But Simon was eager to please his parents. He abided with his father's drinking and mother's carelessness, for they did neither when Simon was present. That behavior was only reserved for Igneus and Valcom. Igneus grew resentful and distant, angry at the world and often did his chores with malice. Valcom was the youngest and the most picked on by his parents and oldest brother, Simon. Since childhood, he was timid and easily sidelined. He would let the rain wash over him, while Igneus would drum with the thunder. Their mother, father, and oldest brother would stay in their house, ignoring nature's fit.

"Cut the log, boy," the command startled Valcom from his wandering thoughts. A large round log was placed standing up in front of him. Valcom looked at the log, then back at his father. The grim man tapped his boot, his eyes red from their recent fever. Valcom knew that he had no way out, that no matter how heavy the axe was, he would have to do what his father commanded. He repositioned the axe in his arms, the fingers circling tight around it, careful with the dull blade.

"Well, go on, boy," his father barked. The little five-year-old boy looked up at his father before he fixed the axe in his arms. He lifted it above his head, teetering as he did so. His arms nearly gave out as he brought the axe down. Unsurprisingly, he missed the log, causing it to fall and roll into the snow. Before Valcom could make sense of what happened, his father's fist hit him across the face. He fell to the ground, clutching his face. A whimper escaped his mouth as the tears started streaming down his cheeks.

"Do you want your family to freeze? Huh, boy?" his father growled, leaning into his face. His breath smelled bitter. Simon approached with an arrogant smile on his pink lips.

"Simon actually cares. Simon's a real man," his father said spitefully before grabbing his chin and pushing it harshly.

Valcom fell to the ground and looked up with blurry eyes.

His older brother eagerly grabbed the axe and carefully propped up the wood before striking it cleanly in two. His father laughed with joy, sharing in the moment. Valcom wiped his tears with the back of his hand as he made his way to their home.

One day, he promised himself that it will be warm and filled with lots of friendly faces. As he entered through the half-opened door, he saw that Igneus was at their little dinner table, clearing away the many smelly glasses, while their mother slept peacefully in her chair, still clutching her 'potion' tightly. Maybe he could turn this place into something where everyone can enjoy their drinks, since that's the most important part.

"Again?" Valcom whispered.

"Always," Igneus breathed, glasses clinking in his hands. "How's father?"

Valcom brushed his hair back with his fingers and turned his head to show his brother where a bruise was forming. Igneus dropped the glasses he was holding and ran over to his brother.

"Let me-"

"No. Doing anything will make it worse."

"Valcom…"

"It was just like when we were younger," Valcom said, wrapping his arms around his knees.

Igneus sat down beside his brother, just as they had done many times before.

"Tell me," Igneus muttered.

As Valcom started recounting the horrid incident, he was interrupted by a loud, glass-shattering voice in his mind telling him to focus on the tasks at hand.

The amber liquid traced the side of the flask, soaking his cracked fingers. "Boy," he whispered, "You took too long."

A young man stood quivering in the roaring gaze of the man lounging in the wooden chair. His clothes stuck to him with sweat as he walked. Yet, the boy still felt freezing from being outside all day. He flexed his calloused fingers at his sides.

"It's cold, and I don't— I can't kill anything. I didn't get the rabbit. I was tired from the march up and down the hill with the sacks of meal," the young man squealed. The old man rose to his full height, the chair squeaking in relief of the absent weight. He reminded the boy of a bear.

"Fool," he seethed, his voice rough as gravel. "Your brother is getting married in a few days' time. You aren't selfish enough to put your own comfort before your brother and future sister, are you?"

"No, Father. But I've been sick for the last couple of days. The cold isn't good for me!"

A sharp sting exploded across Valcom's face, the blow so fierce it knocked him to the ground. His cheek burned and pulsed, the taste of iron pooling on his tongue. From outside, Igneus came charging into the main room, just in time to see their father's shadowed arm lift again for another strike through the windowpane.

"No! You'll only make it worse," Valcom whispered, holding his face.

Simon and their mother entered, alarm tightening their voices.

"Don't fight, Valcom!" Simon shouted, stepping forward. Igneus turned on him, eyes blazing.

"Coward!" he roared, lunging at his brother—but before he could reach him, a massive calloused hand seized him by the back of the neck.

"Your younger brother was being punished for his selfishness," their father snarled.

Igneus struggled like a trapped animal. "You don't know your son at all!" He stomped on his father's boot, but the man held firm, his grip like an iron vice. Igneus shouted and kicked, his cries echoing through the house.

Valcom staggered upright, still dizzy from the strike, his ears ringing. Simon hovered uncertainly nearby, torn between fear and pride.

He was about to speak when a sudden, shattering crash silenced the chaos.

Their mother stood in the doorway, chest heaving, shards of glass and spilled liquor glistening on the wall behind her. Her hand was still raised from the throw.

"You are all selfish!" she cried. "I am tired. There is much to be done before our Simon gets married. Fighting, however deserved or not, accomplishes none of it!"

She swept past them, skirts swishing, muttering something about flowers as she disappeared back into the cold air beyond the door.

The day their parents had died turned out to be the day after Simon's wedding. The air still reeked of spilled wine and smoke from the celebration, the scent turning their stomachs. Igneus buried himself in others' troubles to drown his own. Simon and his new wife soon left for their cottage, planning on reusing materials from the wedding at the funeral.

Valcom… Valcom had finally achieved what he thought he wanted.

With a ragged breath, he stood before his tavern, his life's work—now roaring with flame. Smoke poured through the windows like black ribbons. Sparks and embers burst from his lips as if his rage had taken physical form. The roof caved in with a deafening crack. Tables where friends once sang were devoured by fire, chairs collapsing in the inferno's hungry mouth. He

stood motionless as his home turned to ash, his silhouette trembling in the orange glow. Then, without looking back, Valcom walked toward his new, hollow abode.

****

A stone suddenly smashed through the window, scattering shards across the floor and jolting him from his thoughts. More followed, a rain of rock and glass, the sound like hail striking the castle walls. Rain seeped through the cracks, trailing down in silver ribbons.

Murmuring a spell, Valcom's vision blurred, darkened, then shifted, until he was looking down from the clouds themselves. Below, a sea of figures surged toward the main gate, torches and weapons flashing in the murk.

Valcom smiled faintly.

Vesper à due, a voice hissed in his mind.

From the air, violet fog unfurled, spilling like ink into the crowd. Coughs erupted in unison. Peasants and nobles alike clawed at their throats.

King Cedric fell to his knees, gasping for breath, fingers tearing at his collar as if to carve an opening for air. His crown tilted, his face purpled. Around him, one by one, Sorcerac's people collapsed. An orchestra of choking and despair.

Above them, the architect of their suffering watched impassively, then turned away, as if the spectacle had bored him.

Those who survived crawled on all fours, dragging themselves through the fog toward the gates. The heavy doors groaned and burst open with a thunderous boom, spilling desperate bodies into the clean air.

Valcom left the room, his boots finding purchase on nothing as he strode down the hall toward the keep.

From the highest tower, the land of Sorcerac stretched before him like a painting in ruin. The forests smoldered, the seas frothed with dead fish and sickly green algae. His new dominion was tainted, but perfect, in its devastation.

Then, with his sharpened sight, he noticed movement: four horses racing toward the castle, four cloaked riders bent low over their saddles.

With a sound between a snarl and a prayer, Valcom began to chant:

"Sol mora lonthor riavagh, Sol mora lonthor riavagh, Sol mora lonthor riavagh."

The mud several feet before the horses began to tremble, rippling like the surface of a dark pond as Valcom's voice echoed in the distance. His chants grew louder, raw with fury. He clutched the stones beneath him until they split the skin of his palms, blood mingling with grit.

The earth answered his rage. The sludge began to rise from its slumber, thick clumps twisting together, shaping into grotesque forms. First a torso, then spindly arms, and legs that sagged under their own weight. Their heads were smooth, featureless—save for a faintly glowing purple rune etched into where their foreheads might have been.

Miriana counted quickly as their horses pounded closer. "At least seven," she murmured, her stomach dropping.

"What the heck are those things?" Neel squealed, his voice cracking in panic.

"Something of Valcom's?" Amalia shouted, the wind stealing half her words.

With a sickening splat, one of the creatures lurched forward, then another, gaining momentum with each heavy step. The sound of squelching mud grew louder, faster.

"We run 'em over!" Miriana yelled, kicking her heels into her horse's sides.

The riders surged ahead, a blur of hooves and firelight. As they collided with the advancing horde, the golems flung themselves at the horses, slapping onto their flanks like wet clay. The beasts screamed and reared, throwing the group into chaos.

Igneus growled, drawing a knife. He plunged it into the nearest creature's head. The blade sank deep with a sickening *glarp* and vanished, swallowed whole by the mud.

"What the hell is wrong with you?!" Igneus shouted as the monster kept crawling, his knife and part of his hand still embedded in its skull.

Around him, the scene erupted into madness. Amalia screamed as one of the golems clambered up her horse, tugging at her arm, trying to drag her beneath its churning hooves.

Neel's horse buckled under another, the creature's limbs wrapped around its muzzle. The horse slipped, collapsing in a cry of agony, pinning Neel's leg.

"Argh!" he gasped, trapped.

Another creature reached Miriana, its dripping hand wrapping around her throat. She thrashed, torch flaring wildly. The flame struck the creature's face—steam hissed, and chunks of dirt peeled away, glowing orange. The golem recoiled, screeching in a voice like wind through hollow bones.

"The fire! It's the only thing that can harm them!" Miriana screamed.

One leaped at her from behind, its mud-coated arm locking around her waist. Without thinking, she stabbed the torch backward. The flame met the rune, the creature let out a shriek that seemed to tear the air itself. The creature's head erupted, showering her with shards of burning clay that sliced her cheeks. Her torch guttered out, plunging her into shadow.

Amalia, seeing her friend in distress, swung her torch wildly. Her horse reared, foam and fear flying from its mouth as a golem crawled up its muzzle, smothering its breath. The beast screamed, half mad, as Amalia pressed the torch against the monster's face. The purple glyph flickered, then burst, the creature dissolving into blackened clods that rained to the earth.

Ahead, Miriana shouted, "My torch is out!"

"Miriana!" Amalia cried and hurled her own flame through the air. Miriana caught it, the fire sputtering but alive. She spurred her horse toward Neel, who was choking on mud, the substance seeping into his mouth.

She swung hard, cleaving through the creature's neck. Its head toppled, disintegrating before it hit the ground. The remaining fragments were crushed under their horses' pounding hooves.

Igneus roared, driving his dagger—his beacon—deep into the "What the hells?!" gut of another brute. It exploded into a spray of tiny fragments that sliced the air like glass. He looked around, breathing hard. The others were pale, trembling, but still fighting, still pushing forward.

***

At the castle, Valcom paced his new chamber like a caged beast. The mirror on the wall stood cracked and warped, refusing to show him anything he wished to see. He didn't need it. He knew.

His skin was the color of ash; his cheeks hollowed into caverns. The veins in his hands pulsed yellow beneath paper-thin flesh. He gripped the Black Book so tightly that his knuckles turned white, whispering to it, as if it might whisper back.

Finally, he lifted his gaze to the mirror.

"Oulfa imirgen ay ix!" Valcom bellowed.

The Book writhed in his hands, then melted, oozing into his skin. He gasped as it crawled up his arm, a burning, living ink. The liquid hardened into scales, purple and gleaming like obsidian.

A scream tore from his throat. The transformation spread, his veins glowing gold beneath the new, scaled hide. From his fingertips burst claws—curved and predatory. The flesh at his wrist split, reknitting itself into armor. His body convulsed. Black and yellow blood spilled from his mouth, sizzling on the floor and eating through the stone with a sharp hiss.

Valcom collapsed onto his back, panting. The pain dulled to a pulse, then a perverse pleasure. He clenched his new hand, the talons biting into his palm, black blood dripping between his fingers.

When he finally looked again, his arm was the color of bruised night—purple and plated, his nails dagger-sharp. He bared his teeth in a grotesque grin as he stood.

"They can never take you from me now, beloved," he whispered to the reflection.

In the fractured mirror, his eyes blazed yellow-green, pupils narrowing into serpentine slits. He blinked once, twice, until they softened back to blue, though the sickly tint lingered. He smiled wider. His teeth had become fangs, bright and perfect as ivory blades.

Tilting his head back, Valcom howled, a cry of triumph that shook the rafters.

"They will know," he growled, "just how badly this animal has been wounded."

A chill wind slipped through a crack in the wall, brushing his cheek like a ghost's breath.

"What?" he muttered. The breeze seemed to whisper something in his ear—soft, coaxing, dangerous. He laughed it off. "Only the wind," he told himself, scratching absently at his ear.

He flexed his clawed hand, watching the talons extend and retract with serpentine grace.

"Let the games begin," he whispered. His tongue, now pink and forked, coiled against a fang as he smiled at his reflection. He gave a playful snap at the mirror, chuckling.

But then, deep within him, another voice stirred—a low murmur that told him to stop playing. There was work to be done.

He stood taller, letting the truth sink in: the castle was his. The king's fortress, the queen's chambers, all now silent beneath his reign.

A powerful king, he thought. No, an immortal one.

Behind him, unnoticed, his shadow stretched and twisted—its mouth splitting into a toothy grin, its eyes slitting like his own. It climbed the wall behind him, flickering in the firelight that no one had lit.

****

The cold ocean wind invaded the castle, sweeping dust and ash through the corridors.

Miriana, Igneus, and the others burst through the gates, boots pounding against the marble floors. Their breaths came in ragged bursts. Igneus's red eye darted wildly, searching. Amalia gathered her skirt, leaping over chunks of fallen stone. As they made their way into the castle, they couldn't help but stare in horror at the bodies lying on the ground, their hands at their throats. Amalia let out a squeal of terror as she pointed frozen to a heap on the ground.

"The king," Neel muttered, leaning down to examine the monarch's face.

"We have to keep moving," Igneus commanded.

They entered the destroyed castle, dust and debris fell from the ceiling.

"He must be upstairs," Miriana mused.

After they climbed the stairs, Igneus surveyed the main upstairs hallway as Amalia noticed claw marks carved deep into the marble that led from the staircase down the corridor.

"He must be in a bedroom!" she cried.

They rounded a corner and opened the first door which was torn like fabric with talons and scorch marks seeping into the wood. There he stood, facing the terrace. At his new basilisk like appearance, Miriana and Igneus blanched while Neel and Amalia stood stupefied.

"Valcom, what in the hell is wrong with you?!" Igneus shouted, barely ducking as his brother whirled around, wielding a newly formed claw that slashed through the air.

"I'm freeing myself, brother," Valcom hissed as he walked to the bed frame He then began scaling the wooden bedpost like a feral thing. His limbs moved on all fours, talons scraping the surface, the sound sharp and inhuman.

With a flick of his wrist, his claw flattened and lengthened, curving into an arched blade. He swung his arm back and brought it down in a vicious arc toward his niece. Miriana dove aside just in time—the blade struck marble, shattering it into glittering shards that sliced her temple.

"Igneus!" she gasped.

Her uncle was already charging. His boots thundered against the floor as he lunged for Valcom's back, but Valcom heard the footfalls and struck out with the back of his arm. The blow sent Igneus flying, crashing into the wall with a groan.

Valcom raised the axe again, poised to strike down Miriana where she lay. But when he looked into her terrified face, so young, so familiar, the green serpent's glow in his eyes flickered, fading back into human blue.

"Valcom, what are you doing?" Igneus shouted, staggering upright, narrowly dodging another sweep of his brother's claw.

"I'm freeing myself, brother," Valcom repeated, his voice quieter, colder. He climbed higher along the bedpost, his talons tapping against the wood, the sound like dripping rain.

Miriana rose, sword trembling but outstretched. Igneus stepped beside her, daggers drawn, ready though his hands shook. Neel and Amalia flanked them, torches raised in trembling fists.

Valcom stood out on a balcony framed by fractured moonlight spilling through scattered gray clouds. His expression was unreadable, a crease cutting deep into his brow.

"Brother, please!" Igneus called out, his voice breaking. But Valcom only heard the whispers curling inside his skull, a thousand venomous voices whispering secrets of betrayal.

"You all said you loved me," he breathed, voice trembling, almost childlike. "That you all cared about me."

"We do! Please come back!" Miriana shouted, her voice raw with desperation.

Valcom's eyes were distant and mournful. How could he believe them? How could he believe any of them when they stood there armed against him, blades glinting in the torchlight?

He took a step backward, his heel brushing the threshold of the terrace. A cold night wind swept in, chilling his bare skin and whispering of freedom.

"Valcom, I don't know what you're doing, or what you're planning," Neel pleaded, voice cracking with fear. "We haven't known you long, but you were good to Amalia and me, okay? Would I say that if I didn't care?!?"

Lies. All of it. To Valcom, their words were a poison sweetened with pity. He looked to his brother. Igneus's face carved with anguish, his eyes wet with unfallen tears.

Valcom stepped back again. The air was so cool, so light, so freeing.

"Valcom…" Miriana's voice wavered. She was crying now, really crying, and that startled him. She had never been one to weep. Not as a child, not ever.

Why was she crying?

Pain flared in his skull, sharp and relentless. He doubled over, clutching his head as two voices battled within him—two masters clawing for control. One whispered: Run. Be unchained. The other hissed: Stay. Be safe. Be guarded.

This life has hurt you so, the first voice coaxed. *Why stay chained? They never loved you. Where were they when you suffered?*

Shouts pierced through the haze, muffled and distorted. Valcom blinked, but the world was a blur of light and shadow. Shapes moved—his family, maybe, but they did not come closer. They stayed back.

Because they feared him.

No, the voice insisted, *because they don't care. If they loved you, they'd reach for you. But they won't. They never did. They're scared of you—of what you are. They're jealous. Weak. You're beyond them now. Trust me.*

Valcom turned slowly toward the open air—the cliff disguised as a balcony.

"Valcom," Igneus said softly, climbing the steps with careful, measured movements. "I don't have much in this cruel world. But I can't lose you. You're my flesh and blood. You're my brother."

Valcom's lips trembled. "Yes, you are my brother," he murmured, as if convincing himself. "But what of Simon? He was our brother too. While I struggled, you both fought—like bees and wasps. I was the one between you, the mediator. I kept you safe. I did every chore under the gods-forsaken sun for a mother and father who never loved me." His voice cracked into a hiss. "I raised you both when I was still a child myself."

Igneus's mind raced, heart hammering. "What of your destiny?! Isn't it yours to carve out?! Whose destiny is this if you have to cling to that cursed book?! What of Miriana's uncle? My brother? "

What destiny did any of them have? Destiny? Valcom almost laughed. What destiny had ever been his? His parents' marriage had been a misery; his childhood, servitude. Simon had vanished, his wife with him. And their child, poor, forsaken Miriana—what had she been given but scraps of love and the shadow of her uncles' guilt?

He glanced toward her now, though his vision swam. Her figure wavered like a reflection on water. What destiny could she possibly have?

He thought of Igneus again, his brother who'd joined killers and called them family. What destiny did any of them have? Perhaps there was no destiny at all. Perhaps life was only what you took by force.

Valcom turned away, facing the open dark. The sea wind tugged at his hair, the salt air sharp in his lungs. The voices quieted, all but one.

A single, irresistible whisper now filled his mind

He tilted his head slightly, eyes empty. "You have already lost him," the voice said.

Valcom set off running, his bare feet slapping against the marble, echoing through the vast hall like thunder. Behind him came the clamor of pursuit, shouts, pleas, the sound of boots and panic.

"Valcom!" they cried.

He hesitated for the briefest moment, just enough for their voices to reach him—desperate, pleading, almost convincing. For an instant, he wanted to believe them. That they truly wanted him to have a destiny… his own destiny.

But no. They were too late. They had always been too late.

A warmth brushed against his mind, a caress, gentle as a lover's hand. It soothed the burning behind his eyes. *I care for you,* it whispered. *And you care for me. We are one.*

Power surged through his veins, filling him with something divine. He felt his immortal strength rising

He climbed the terrace rail, planted a clawed hand on the stone, and vaulted over.

The world seemed to freeze as his family skidded to a halt at the ledge.

"Valcom!" Miriana screamed.

But instead of plummeting, his body rose.

With a sound like tearing silk, his back split open. Bone and sinew burst outward. He screamed as vast wings unfurled from his shoulders. Their membranes glowed a translucent violet in the dawn, each motion slick and wet, veins pulsing beneath the light. The leathery expanse caught the wind, spreading wider, wider still—so massive they seemed to pierce the clouds themselves.

Valcom soared upward, his scream curdling into a triumphant roar.

Then he twisted midair, turning his gaze back toward the figures below. His chest expanded, and a torrent of fire spiraled from his mouth, a vortex of molten gold and violet flame that screamed toward the party.

"Down!" Igneus roared.

They threw themselves to the ground as the blast struck, heat washing over them in a wave that scorched the tiles.

Valcom tilted his great wings upward, catching an updraft, and shot into the air. He clung to the high dome of the ceiling, claws digging into the stone. His monstrous and winged shadow spread across the chamber walls.

A roar erupted from him, shaking dust loose from the rafters.

"Oh god," Igneus choked, staring upward, as they all jumped to their feet.

Sunlight filtered through the broken roof above, painting the chamber in amber hues. Valcom's silhouette moved across the ceiling, like one of the great reptilian beasts from the tales of their youth.

Then, with another deafening roar, he dove.

His claws extended, reaching for the first target in his sight—Miriana.

"Miriana!" Igneus bellowed. He lunged, tackling her just as Valcom struck. The two crashed to the floor as Valcom slammed into the tiles, cracking them like ice. Igneus, with a scream, tackled his brother.

Fists colliding with his opponent's face. A *crack* sounded as knuckles collided with bones.Acidic blood began to pour out of Valcom's nose as he smiled. The smell of burning flesh filled the air as Ignues clutched his now burning arm in surprise. Taking his chance, Valcom pushed his brother over and clawed him over and over again as Igneus struggled to clasp his knife in his belt. Valcom's claws slashed into his sibling's flesh as Igneus tried to escape.

"Hey!" Miriana shouted from where she laid.

Valcom turned to her and rose slowly, wings folding around his body like a shroud. Then, with a sudden burst of movement, he lunged again on all fours, galloping across the floor with terrifying speed.

Amalia darted forward, trying to intercept. Miriana and Igneus scrambled to their feet, running, but Valcom was too fast.

Neel grabbed the nearest object, a shattered wooden chair, and with a shout, charged.

Valcom reached Miriana first, his claw sweeping in a blinding arc. She stumbled back, but not far enough. The talons raked across her face, blood splattering the marble. The gashes tore straight through the "cursed" mark that had haunted her since birth.

Her sword belt was ripped from her waist—Valcom flung the blade aside with a snarl.

"Uncle, stop!" she screamed, grasping his wrists, trying to hold him back.

From behind, Neel swung the chair with all his strength. It splintered against Valcom's back, exploding into pieces.

Valcom howled, whirling on the boy, his eyes burning gold.

Igneus, dazed and bleeding, rose to his feet. Fury roared through him like fire. He snatched up Miriana's discarded sword and charged.

"VALCOM!"

Valcom leaped toward Neel, but Igneus met him midair, swinging the blade in a desperate arc. The steel carved across Valcom's face, leaving a searing line from cheek to jaw. Yellow blood spattered the floor, sizzling as it hit the stone.

Valcom stumbled back, clutching his face. The blood dripped between his fingers in slow, heavy drops.

"Valcom, I didn't mean—" Igneus stammered, lowering the sword.

A groan from behind drew his attention—Miriana lay motionless, her friends rushing to her side.

Igneus's expression hardened. The creature before him was no longer his brother.

With a snarl of grief and rage, he gripped the sword tighter and charged.

CHAPTER TEN

The brothers launched themselves at each other. Igneus's strike glanced harmlessly off Valcom's newly hardened hide, the impact sounding like stone on iron. Valcom huffed a low, mirthless laugh and straightened to his full height, his eyes glinting with something both foreign and ancient.

The chill of the castle seeped through the walls, making the fine hairs on the back of Valcom's neck stand stiff. He inhaled once, deeply, as if drawing breath from the marrow of the earth itself. Then he spoke the words that rose unbidden from the darkest corners of his memory.

"Ad altiera lendo."

As the final syllable left his tongue, his voice roughened, deepened—echoing through the chamber like a cavernous bell. His tunic tore as jagged scales burst through skin and cloth alike, unfurling into a sheen of violet armor that shimmered in the dim torchlight. The transformation spread like wildfire—along his jaw, across his arms, until his very breath hissed with heat. A dry click of his forked tongue sparked the air with a brief flash of flame.

"This is your last chance," Valcom bellowed.

The words hung heavy in the silence that followed. His lips curled into a small, cruel smile before he parted them again.

Fire rolled from his mouth in a roaring surge. The blaze struck forward like a living creature, illuminating the vaulted ceiling in a hellish glow. Igneus leapt without thought, placing himself before the others. The inferno consumed him. His sleeves blackened and curled against his skin; flesh bubbled beneath as the searing heat clawed through his defenses. He gritted his teeth against the agony until, mercifully, the torrent faltered—Valcom gasping through heaving, smoke-filled breaths.

When the flames subsided, Valcom stood larger than before, his silhouette warped and monstrous. His feet had split and thickened into clawed talons like an alligator's, scraping against the flagstones. His face stretched long and narrow, scales glimmering like wet amethyst. The very air of the chamber shimmered, growing thick with heat.

"You see, brother? The power I possess?" His tone was half triumph, half venom. "No—you choose to be weak."

With a violent motion of his arm, he cast his hand toward the three companions. A wave of unseen force slammed into them, pinning them against the wall.

"Igne—" Amalia tried to cry out, but her voice was swallowed whole. The air itself seemed stolen from their lungs; they struggled soundlessly, eyes wide in panic.

Valcom let out a quiet, satisfied chuckle and let his arm fall. Yet his enemies remained suspended, helpless.

Igneus staggered toward his niece, seizing her shoulders, trying desperately to wrench her free. It was like trying to pull against a hurricane. The invisible wind held her fast, her limbs rigid as marble.

"Free them!" Igneus begged, his voice cracking. Sweat and tears mingled on his blistered face.

"Why?" Valcom's voice was almost tender now, almost amused. "Why, when I finally hold the power and the adoration I have always craved?" He turned away from them with deliberate indifference, as though their struggle were no more than children pestering him for sweets after supper.

"Who gives you this adoration?" Igneus rasped, still clawing at the invisible bindings. His desperation was raw, trembling.

Valcom laughed—a dark, delighted sound that filled the hall. "Who said it was a who, dear brother?"

Igneus's eyes darted toward his brother, then back to his trapped companions, their faces pale and straining. "The only way to unbind them is to stop Valcom," he muttered. "He's angry. And that makes him all the more dangerous." He looked to his family once more, his voice dropping to a whisper. "I've got to get the book. Somehow."

He raised his voice. "Where is the book, Valcom?"

Valcom had drifted to the balcony, where an armchair—once rich red velvet—had been dragged near the open doors. He reclined there, gazing out over the sinking sun, head propped on his hand. He tapped his foot idly, humming an absent tune, utterly unconcerned as Igneus approached behind him.

Rage welled in Igneus like molten metal. He strode forward, seized the back of the armchair, and spun it sharply around.

Valcom met his gaze with an impassive expression. He ceased humming, folding his hands over his knee with deliberate calm. Igneus's face burned red with fury and grief, the heat of his anger nearly matching the fire that had scorched him moments ago.

Valcom's lips curved slowly into a smirk.

"Where is the book, Valcom?" Igneus demanded again, his voice rough with emotion.

Valcom only smiled wider. He rose unhurried and unflinching and raised his right hand. The scales glinted up to his elbow, each one edged sharp as glass, and from his fingertips extended claws like blades.

Igneus's stomach dropped as realization began to dawn.

"I don't understand," he whispered. "Where is the book? What have you done to your arm?"

Valcom regarded his taloned hand as one might admire a precious relic, his gaze filled with something disturbingly akin to love.

"Valcom!" Igneus's voice cracked through the room.

Valcom's head lifted lazily, "Yes, dear brother?"

"The book," Igneus said through gritted teeth. "Where is the book that you are so obsessed with?"

Valcom rolled his eyes, flicking his scaled hand in front of Igneus's face. "I have already answered you, brother."

The color drained from Igneus's face. "Are you telling me… that the book is now your arm?"

Valcom chuckled. "My, perhaps the round stone does possess some sharp edges after all."

"H-how… that's not possible," Igneus stammered, stumbling backward until he nearly tripped over the polished table behind him. Disbelief overwhelmed his senses.

Valcom stepped forward, the floor creaking beneath his weight. "Oh, but it makes perfect sense. The book was never meant to be read—it was meant to be absorbed. Its language binds not the tongue, but the soul. With it, I command all that moves and breathes around me."

He spread his arms wide, his voice swelling with fervor. "The words are ancient, Igneus. They are threads of fate themselves, and I—" he smiled faintly "—I am their loom."

For a moment, he gazed at his scaled hands with something almost tender. "They give me such comfort. Like a hearth, warm and soft."

Igneus scoffed, unable to contain the bitterness boiling within him.

Valcom's head snapped toward him, eyes narrowing to slits. "Do you have something to say, dear brother?"

"It doesn't make sense," Igneus muttered, shaking his head.

"What doesn't?" Valcom's voice slithered low, the hiss of serpents coiling beneath his words.

"How do the words—however ancient, in whatever language—do that?" Igneus struggled to form the question, his mind caught between disbelief and dread.

Valcom tilted his head back and unleashed a sharp, barking laugh; a wild, feral sound that echoed off the stone walls and made Igneus flinch. It was the laughter of something no longer fully human.

"It's ancient," Valcom said, eyes bright and fevered. "Older than kingdoms, older than gods. Perhaps as old as time itself." He turned to his brother, his expression radiant, almost childlike in its mania. "It's magic," he whispered, savoring the word.

Igneus gave a short, disbelieving laugh that faltered when he saw the flex of Valcom's taloned hand— the way the claws slid out and retracted again, restless, eager.

"Magic?" Igneus echoed. " If it is magic, then why has no one used it? Why did it vanish from the world?"

Valcom's tone softened, "It was hidden—guarded. Like a well sealed from mortal hands. Or perhaps from the universe itself. It—"

He stopped mid-sentence, eyes flicking upward. His posture stiffened. For a moment, his gaze grew distant, listening to something unheard.

"That's quite enough," he said finally, his voice abrupt and cold. "No more questions." He cradled his scaled arm as though soothing a lover. "I could not bear to part from it, or to see it wielded by another. It speaks to me now. My thoughts are its own, and its voice fills the quiet places in my mind."

He clasped his clawed hands together in delight, his smile unnervingly serene. Igneus gripped the edge of the desk behind him to keep steady. His stomach turned, the room spinning faintly.

"This is not you," he whispered hoarsely. "I don't know who this is... but it's not you, Valcom." Igneus tried to bide his time for his family as he thought of a plan.

Valcom's expression twisted. His lips peeled back to reveal a new line of dagger-like teeth. The torchlight caught on their edges. Igneus shuddered. Behind them, Neel gasped—the pressure in the air rising with Valcom's fury.

"This is me," Valcom spat. "This is who I have always been beneath the pretense. This book—" he raised his arm high "—has freed me from the shackles I forged for myself."

His eyes flared, irises burning into a brilliant, venomous green. The color spread inward from the corners until his pupils narrowed to slits.

"Remove it," Igneus said sharply.

Valcom laughed, a deep, unsettling sound. "Excuse me?"

"You heard me. It's poisoning you—it's twisting you. You've chained yourself to another captor. This is madness!"

The words had barely left his lips before Valcom struck him. The back of his scaled hand cracked across Igneus's face, sending him staggering into the vanity. He caught himself on trembling arms, gasping.

"Madness?" Valcom thundered, his voice filling every corner of the room. "This book—this reward— was given to me for enduring all the pain this wretched world forced upon me. To remind me that it was not for nothing! That I am more than a man shoveling filth for ungrateful bastards!"

His eyes blazed with a hatred so fierce Igneus barely recognized him. *Who is this graveyard of my brother?* he thought numbly.

"This is a gift from the stars themselves!" Valcom cried, throwing his arms skyward.

Before he could rise higher in his mania, Igneus lunged, tackling him to the ground. They crashed against the cold stone, the impact shaking the table beside them.

Valcom recovered instantly, his strength unnatural. He twisted, pinning Igneus beneath him. His claws tore through cloth and flesh alike, raking crimson lines down his brother's chest.

"Stop!" Igneus hissed, gripping Valcom's wrist. His hands slipped on the blood, slick and hot. Valcom drove his knee down hard, striking Igneus square in the chest atop the fresh wounds.

The trio up against the wall moaned with protest, but the pressure keeping them there was far stronger than their determination to come to their friend's aid. The stress against them forced them to watch their companions battle.

Igneus groaned, the sound muffled by the weight pressing on him. Then Valcom pressed his thumb against Igneus's marble eye, the pressure sharp and merciless. A wicked smile curled on his lips.

Igneus, desperate, drew the dagger from his belt and slashed upward.

He hadn't meant to cut deeply, only to make him stop. But the blade bit, and flesh parted.

Valcom reeled backward with a sharp cry, clutching his face. Between his fingers, thick yellow blood seeped and dripped to the floor.

Igneus scrambled to his feet, the dagger falling from his shaking hand. "I'm sorry! I'm so sorry, I—"

A sudden chill stopped him. The temperature dropped so fast his breath came out in mist.

"Valcom?" he whispered.

Valcom lowered his hands slowly. The wound gaped hideously across his cheek—skin flayed, a flap hanging loose. The sight froze Igneus where he stood.

Valcom's chuckle was hollow. *"Illian saem eth draven vesp,"* he murmured.

The air turned glacial. Frost crept along the stones. Igneus's breath came quick and shallow as he watched the blood flow backward—up the cheek, into the wound. The torn flesh drew together, knitting, sealing itself smooth.

Moments later, the gash was gone.

Valcom touched his face, smiled, and exhaled a satisfied sigh. "It takes some getting used to," he said gently. "But one accepts it quickly."

He stepped forward, extending his hand. Igneus backed away, shaking his head.

"Do you see now, brother? The power I possess? No pain can touch me. No force can harm me. I am beyond it all." His voice dropped to a reverent whisper. "I am untouchable."

Igneus could not speak. His throat locked around the words.

"Igneus," Valcom said softly, "I can give you a portion." His eyes drifted, scanning the room, to the overturned chair, the scattered table, as though searching for something unseen. He paused, listening again to the silence. Then his gaze snapped back, sharp as a blade.

His eyes now gleamed with a predatory yellow-green light. The pupils were slit, narrow, and cold.

"Imagine it," he breathed. "No fear. No weakness. No sleepless nights or trembling hands. Together, we could make the world kneel. We could be eternal."

Igneus surged forward, seized his brother by the shoulders, and shook him violently. "This isn't you!"

"This is me!" Valcom roared. "I offer you what men and kings only dream of, and you insult me with your pity? You claim to know me?" His voice broke with fury. "We could have it all, Igneus! Something Simon never lived to see!"

The name struck like a bell. Igneus's breath caught.

"I don't want this," he whispered. "Simon wouldn't have wanted it either. You are my brother. I know that much."

Valcom's face twisted. With a guttural snarl, he gripped Igneus's throat and lifted him from the floor. His talons bit into flesh.

Igneus choked and kicked, eyes bulging. Foam gathered at his lips as he clawed weakly at the scaled hand. For a heartbeat, he met Valcom's gaze, and for that fleeting instant, his brother's eyes flickered blue.

The grip loosened. Igneus dropped like a stone to the cold, unfeeling floor, coughing and gasping.

Valcom turned away, stepping out onto the balcony. He rested one hand on the marble balustrade, the setting sun bathing his violet scales in a burnished glow.

"The offer stands only for a few moments more," he said quietly. "After that, my patience ends." He paused, his voice softening with something almost mournful. "I do not wish to face the world alone, brother. I would have you beside me—as it once was."

Igneus, trembling, rose slowly to his feet, one hand clutching his bruised throat. His voice came out hoarse, but steady.

"I won't believe this is you."

"I am exactly who everyone made me. This is the fate the island dealt me," Valcom spat, each word a bitter stone cast into the still air.

Igneus moved with desperate speed. From his belt he snatched a knife and sprang, the blade raised over his head. He slammed into his brother; steel met marble with a harsh, ringing chip as the dagger struck the floor. Valcom shoved, his clawed hand driving against Igneus's ribs, and the elder brother skidded across the flagstones, skin scraping and breath ragged. Valcom lunged; Igneus was up, and then down again beneath a crushing weight. The regretful assassin felt claws sink into his shoulders. Ice-cold talons bit through cloth and skin. He screamed and, in blind pain, thrust the knife upward into the arm that held him.

Yellow blood poured like oil. Valcom howled, the sound animal and wrenching, and ripped the blade free with a grunt. The knife clattered to the floor.

Around them, the three; Miriana, Neel, and Amalia, strained and bucked against the invisible gale that pinned them. Their faces were white masks of terror; their chests rose and fell with every shuddering breath Valcom took. They had only eyes to watch the wrestle of brothers, helpless to intervene.

"Illian saem eth dr—arh!" Valcom gasped, voice torn as Igneus hauled at his brother's leg and dragged him down. Igneus scrambled for the fallen blade, fingers slick with blood. Valcom's one good hand closed on a fist of hair, yanking Igneus back; the two men tumbled, sliding on the pooling blood that made the flagstones treacherous.

For a frantic moment Igneus straddled Valcom, pinning his arms under his knees. He pressed the knife to the seam where scale met flesh, raised it high—intention pure and terrible. Then Valcom chanted low, and with a force like a thrown boulder Igneus was flung backward. He struck the wall; the knife flew from his grasp and spun away. He slumped down the stone, breath fizzling from him.

Valcom muttered under his breath. A vanity by the wall shuddered and launched itself across the room, crashing down atop Igneus with a sickening thud. The tray of mirror and glass exploded into glittering rain; shards caught in the blood and the sweat on Igneus's brow. He gasped, the air burning his lungs, eyes stinging with splinters and salt.

Valcom padded over with the slow, arrogant grace of a predator. He plucked the knife up from the floor and toyed with it between his claws, watching the blade tilt and drink the poisoned yellow blood. The hem of his cloak whispered like a serpent's tail.

"I always thought seeing me bleed would wound you more than it would wound me," he said softly, stepping closer until the words were a rasp in Igneus's ear. "You, the savior—big brother, the hero. Did you never feel inadequate under Simon's shadow as I did under yours?" He drew his eyes across Igneus's face, hungry for reaction.

Igneus only breathed, the world tilting. Valcom crouched and, with an intimacy that made Igneus's skin crawl, pressed his lips near his ear.

"I will kill you," he whispered, cold and certain. "To show you how strong this world has made me."

Igneus lunged with the last of his strength. Valcom moved with the speed of a striking viper—he found the fallen knife and sliced across Igneus's cheek. The scream tore out of him, raw and animal. Valcom shoved the vanity aside and forced Igneus flat upon the stone. He planted a knee in his brother's chest and dropped the blade away as if it were no longer needed. Igneus clawed at his face, fingers slick with dark red that seeped through his spread digits.

Valcom's free claw sank into Igneus's neck. Not to cut, but to pin, to hold, to make a point. He pushed every sliver of contempt and triumph into that grip, and then, almost as an afterthought, he released the enchantment that had bound the others. The gust that imprisoned Miriana and the others slacked, though the force still made them stay there; air rushed back into their lungs like the tide returning.

"I offered you an ultimatum," Valcom said, voice wrapped in something like a ceremony. He rose and stepped back, letting the gravity of the act settle between them. "You refused and insulted me. Your arrogance has been punished. I hope never to see you again. Should we meet twice, it will be your heart that bleeds."

A droplet of what looked suspiciously like wine of life fell from Igneus's face and splashed to the flagstones. Blood blurred his sight. He felt a heavy silence descend—then the clink of glass under his hand.

Crawling, with one hand pressed to his ruined eye and the other dragging him, Igneus reached the vanity's wreck. Shards jutted like tiny teeth from the floor. With a trembling hand he picked one and, through tears and grit, peeled his fingers back from his face to look. A great rent crossed his cheek; his marble eye had been forced deeper into its socket. He worked the cold piece of glass like a surgeon's tool, easing the marble back toward its place until the socket no longer felt empty and foreign. Blood ran hot. He tore a strip of tunic and mopped at the wound, stanching as best he could.

Slowly, he rose. The room spun. He steadied himself on the wall and limped, each step a small betrayal.

Valcom watched him with a hunger that made the air sick. His voice was low, a growl as he advanced toward Miriana, who remained pinned like an insect in some cruel collector's box.

"You know the sting of neglect, child," Valcom crooned, circling her. "Humans cling to superstition. Your birthmark—a curse—was a sign they could not bear. They sailed away and left you in the wake." He offered his hand with grand, theatrical compassion.

Miriana recoiled. Her face, streaked with dust and fear, said what words did not. "No," she whispered. "You're sick. You're not well, Valcom." She turned her face away in disgust.

His smile flickered, then soured. A shadow, enormous and scaled, unfurled behind him in the last of the dying light. It was an impression, perhaps, of draconian breadth rather than substance. "Do you all think me ill?" he demanded, as if to the room itself. "Because I have been freed from the obligations of others? Because I can finally enact the justice that was denied me?"

Igneus pushed himself up to a standing position, each step a slow, grim determination. "Your family loved you," he said, voice quivering but firm.

"They only hurt me," Valcom snarled.

"All those who hurt you are gone, Valcom," Igneus said. "You don't have to fear them anymore."

Valcom's smirk widened. He lifted a hand—pupils narrow, serpent-bright—and clicked his forked tongue. Smoke curled from his lips. He spread his wings in a sudden, dreadful sweep; they were broad and leathery, casting a huge shadow that swallowed the stairwell. With a whip of his tail, he struck. Igneus was hurled backwards as if flung by some massive hand. His head cracked against the marble and the stars rushed in his vision.

He hit the floor with a groan and lay there, every heartbeat ringing loud in his ears.

After the tension had been strained, Miriana used the surplus of her strength to leap down from the wall, freeing her sword from where it hung beside her. Valcom fell to his arms, bracing himself like a beast ready to strike. With a guttural cry, fire erupted from his mouth and swept toward his niece.

She swung the sword around and raised it upright. Her uncle's flames struck it and split apart, the steel flaring with a faint blue glow at its edges. With a fierce slash, she diverted the torrent into the wall. Paintings blistered and turned a sickly blue as the oils bubbled and burned, erasing centuries of memory.

Neel and Amalia tore themselves from the wall as Valcom rose again, his fingertips pulsing, green and violet light alternating between them like the beat of an unholy heart.

Neel charged and leapt onto Valcom's back, locking his legs around his torso and yanking hard on his head. The wretch staggered backwards.

Amalia ran to Igneus, sliding to her knees. She lifted his head into her lap, shaking him gently, her voice trembling as she called his name.

"Miriana!" Neel shouted. "Get the book!"

Fire burst again from Valcom's mouth, the roar of it shaking the room. Between the blasts, he muttered, the syllables of a dying language tangled with smoke. Furniture and trinkets ripped themselves from the ground, swirling like a storm around him. They hurled through the air at his attackers. A candelabrum struck Neel and clung to him like a living thing.

"Miriana!"

She hesitated just long enough to feel the weight of what she was about to do. Then she drew a breath, purging every thought that threatened to bind her. With a cry that shook the rafters, she ran at her uncle.

"Amalia, duck!" she commanded.

Amalia bent low over Igneus's body as Miriana vaulted off her friend's shoulder, launching herself into the air. Her blade flashed high above her head.

Valcom screamed. Neel still pulled at his head, holding him in distraction as Valcom raised his hand, too late, to shield himself. Time stilled.

The sound of a saber cut through the fire's roar. Valcom looked down—and saw, with slow horror, the yellow blood gushing from his severed stump.

He did not at first realize what had happened. The others watched in stunned silence as his arm fell to the ground with a soft, dreadful thud. The talon curled upon itself, shriveling, sizzling. The smell of burning flesh thickened the air.

Before their eyes, the arm charred, its shape collapsed and thinned until what remained upon the floor was not flesh at all, but a singed, smoking version of The Black Book.

Neel crept closer and nudged it with the toe of his boot. Embers stirred, flaring into white-hot flame that shot up to the ceiling. All turned away, shielding their eyes. When the crackling faded, a mound of ash lay where the book had been.

Deprived of its source, the dark power withered instantly—starved to dust before them. Valcom, who had fed from the same corruption, fell to the floor, drained and trembling.

"Uncle!" Miriana cried, sliding to his side.

Igneus stirred at the sound. Groaning, he rose from Amalia's lap, and arms around each other's shoulders, they approached the kneeling girl and the pale form of Valcom.

Yellow blood from the stump deepened to orange as his body began to change back. Scales dissolved into skin; the tail reformed as the trailing edge of his cloak. His face flattened, more human again. Only the missing arm and the dimming eyes remained as proof of what he had become.

Valcom tried to sit up, but a soft hand on his chest pushed him gently back. "What… happened?" he whispered, the words ragged.

Igneus knelt beside him, leaning on Amalia for support. "You mean you don't remember?" he asked quietly.

Valcom swallowed. "No. I remember everything… leading up to now." His voice cracked.

Miriana bowed her head and rested it on his chest, feeling the faint rise and fall beneath her cheek.

"You will be all right, Valcom," Igneus said softly.

Valcom's dull eyes found his brother's. "I'm—" He broke off with a wrenching cough and sat up suddenly, gasping for breath. Miriana pulled back in alarm. He coughed again, violently, and when he finally sank back, his eyes had turned vacant. The last light had gone from them.

Amalia gave a small, choked wail and buried her face in Neel's chest, letting Igneus go. Her brother held her close, pressing his brow to her shoulder.

"You can finally rest, brother," Igneus murmured, voice breaking.

Miriana stayed kneeling, tears streaming silently as Igneus spoke to her—his words soft and practical, something about burial and peace. Neel lifted Valcom by the shoulders while Igneus limped forward to take his brother's legs. Amalia was behind him with a hand square on his back to steady him.

"Miriana," Igneus said gently, "I think we should bury him at the tree."

The words broke her. A gasp escaped her lips, followed by a flood of tears that gleamed in the dim light.

Neel and Igneus carried his younger brother through the doorway. They all began to bow their heads in mourning. Miriana remained for a long moment, then heard her name called from the hall. Amalia returned, lifted her gently by the shoulders, and helped her to her feet. Miriana wept into her friend's hair as they walked out together. Four figures moving down the corridor in silence, a miniature funeral procession.

At the family's tree, Igneus laid Valcom down at the roots. Silent tears glistened on his face. Miriana could scarcely bear to look; her uncle seemed older than she had ever seen him. Together, she and Igneus drove their shovels into the earth.

"Not too deep," Amalia murmured. "He never did like the dark."

Igneus gave her a fragile smile. Hours passed. At last, a shallow grave was ready. Neel turned away, sobbing into his arm. Amalia laid a steadying hand on his shoulder.

Miriana stared down at the hollow in the ground. Her face was still and her eyes were wide and glimmering. Igneus lowered his brother in and began to cover him with soil.

"I hope you have found peace, brother," he whispered. "I promise I will search for it as well."

At those words, Miriana broke. She fell to her knees, covering her face as her sobs shook her body. Her family gathered beside her in the grass. Together they wept beneath the ancient tree, until at last the outline in the earth blurred through their tears.

EPILOGUE

"What are we to do with the library?" Miriana asked.

Her voice broke the quiet like a pebble dropped into still water. Around her, the council chamber, which was once a dining hall, still smelled faintly of smoke and sawdust. Dust drifted through the sunbeams, cutting across the cracked glass windows.

She sat straight-backed, her several salmon-colored scars catching the light like faded threads of fire. Her faithful sword hung at her hip, its hilt polished but worn smooth from her hand. Strapped to her thigh was a small book in a purple leather holster—the date of Valcom's passing carved into its spine in her careful hand.

It had been months since the world had steadied, months since she had stopped waking expecting blood or thunder. The time had given her something new—an affection for things she'd once dismissed: the birthmark at her temple, the family she still had, and even the ghosts of those who had left her behind.

Across from her, Igneus, Neel, and Amalia sat at the great round wooden table—its surface gouged by years of kings and their secrets. The twins bore only faint reminders of their battles now, pale cuts and bruises fading from their faces. Amalia's white dress deepened to green at the hem, like the sea meeting the forest. Neel wore dark leather over his brown tunic, his posture alert but uncertain.

The others gathered. The merchant, the artisan, the fishmonger, and the priest formed a mismatched circle of power and consequence. For a long moment, no one spoke.

"What library?" asked the merchant finally, his tone clipped, defensive.

Igneus's mechanical eye whirled toward him with a soft hum. The man visibly shrank under its crimson gleam. Igneus had grown stronger since the fall, but his scars had multiplied—one long and pink ran from cheekbone to jaw. His hair, once long, was now cut short with streaks of white, and a restless stubble shadowed his chin.

He offered the merchant a weary smile, though his voice carried the weight of command. "There was a library beneath the late family's throne room," he said. "We're still cataloging what was found—making sure there isn't another book like The Black Book hidden among the wreckage."

The words fell heavy on the table. Even now, months later, the name brought an uneasy silence.

Valcom's funeral had been quiet. He was buried beneath the great Ele tree, the one where Miriana used to read and train, where the grass had sprung up quickly. It was believed by the family that the tree's roots encircled him, holding him fast in death as in life. A shard of timber from his tavern rested with him, the last piece of his beginnings.

Miriana still visited, though she never knew what to say. Sometimes she whispered to the grave, sometimes she stood there for hours, her hand resting on the bark. She told herself she was searching for the right words, something worthy of his soul, if he had one left to hear her.

Igneus had since proposed a new order, a council, rather than a throne. A body of those who had survived, those who understood, and those who held sway over the island's trade. The people called them "the heroes" now, half in reverence, half in relief. He thought the title was foolish, but he didn't correct them.

The island itself was mending, cautiously. The stench of dead fish and rot had long been scrubbed from the shores. The sea, once fouled with foam, had begun to breathe again. Shipworkers said it might be fishable within the month.

The castle rose again from its skeleton, but its heart—the secret chamber, the library—remained untouched. No one could agree what to do with it, or what the castle should become when the work was done. Some whispered of reopening the royal quarters; others wanted to turn it into a hall of memory. None would admit their fear aloud that the past might crawl back out of the stones.

The council, save for Miriana and her kin, still feared coups and curses. They feared the unseen.

"Based on what you've told us about The Black Book, who is to say there aren't more like it?" the merchant pressed. His name, Miriana recalled faintly, was Remus.

Miriana leaned forward, resting her chin on her knuckles. Her eyes studied him, his balding head, the dark skin polished with sweat, the fine blue and purple satin of his clothes. A man who loved wealth more than wisdom.

"In truth," she said evenly, "We don't know. From all we've gathered, there was only one."

"We don't know anything," argued Father Serena. The priest's gold-trimmed tunic glimmered as he gestured sharply. "We didn't even know the first Book existed—and now it's gone!"

Across the table, the artisan Decimus lifted her head. Her tight curls fell into her eyes, but she ignored them, fingers idly brushing the tiny bells that adorned her scarlet dress.

"The Book confirms the witches existed," she said quietly, almost reverently. "How are we to move forward now? Their covens won't take kindly to this, to the destruction of their artifact. Especially not Queen Vivian's."

The name hung in the air like a gust of cold wind.

Neel coughed softly, the sound breaking through the hush that had settled over the council chamber. His sister shifted beside him, the fabric of her dress whispering against the wood. Neel ran a nervous hand through his dirt-brown hair before finding his voice.

"We've been discussing," he began, glancing briefly at Miriana and Igneus, "and obviously nothing can be decided without the council's approval, but we believe sending an exploration party into the woods would be our best chance. A scouting party, if you will."

He rose halfway from his chair, trying to lend weight to his words. But when no one else moved, he faltered, his stance wobbling awkwardly. Heat crept up his neck, and he sat down again, the wood creaking under him.

The room fell quiet. All eyes turned to him. Remus's mouth twitched as if preparing to speak, but Amalia's voice cut through first, steady and clear.

"This would be for safety," she said, her tone deliberate. "There will be no battles and no conflicts, only observation. Decimus is right. The Book's existence confirms that magic is real, and likely older than any of us know. We need to understand it. Learn its history. But *peacefully*."

She pressed her thumbs and forefingers together, drawing a straight line through the air in front of her as if slicing through invisible tension to emphasize the point.

Father Serena's gaze swept across the table, meeting each of theirs in turn before resting on Amalia again. He inhaled deeply, preparing to speak, but Remus, ever impatient, leaned forward first.

"I think it's an excellent idea," he declared, a faint smirk forming. "We could forge alliances, new trade, new knowledge. With these discoveries, Sorcerac could finally progress, rebuild, and think of the—"

"Wealth," came a low, gravelly interruption.

The group turned. The fishmonger, Adamaris, who had dragged his chair as far from the others as the round table would allow, sat with his arms crossed. His skin was rough and red from years in the sun, his white beard hanging in wild curls over his navy shirt.

"That's what you were going to say," he muttered, pointing a thick finger toward the merchant. "And don't act so pious, Father Serena. You're no better, taking coins from the poor and calling it salvation. If we're doing this, it needs to be for the right reasons. Not greed. Not glory."

Father Serena flushed crimson and looked down, his fingers picking at the edge of the table. Remus sighed loudly and dropped his head into his palm, looking theatrically bored.

Igneus cleared his throat, the faint hum of his mechanical eye filling the silence. "Enough," he said. "Are we agreed, then? That we send an expedition, not to fight, but to learn? To understand what remains of the witches, and the truth of the island's history with magic?"

The tension in the air pulsed. Then, one by one, hands began to rise.

Father Serena hesitated, his hand wavered before finally lifting. Decimus's hand followed a moment later, her bracelets chiming softly. Soon, all hands were raised.

"Then it's settled," Miriana said, her voice firm but calm. She glanced at Igneus, who nodded once in approval. "We'll prepare for the expedition and depart in a month's time."

"Meeting adjourned," the group chimed in unison.

She exhaled, the faintest smile tugging at her lips, before confirming, "Meeting adjourned."

Chairs scraped against the floor as the council dispersed into the unfinished halls of the castle. The scent of plaster and sea salt lingered in the air. Neel lingered behind, his hand darting out to catch Igneus's arm as he passed.

Miriana paused at the doorway, her eyes narrowing slightly, but her uncle shook his head with a small, reassuring smile. "Go on," he said gently.

She nodded and slipped out, her footsteps fading into the echoing corridors.

When they were alone, Igneus turned to Neel. "What is it?"

Neel hesitated, his words gathering slowly. "We never talked about the queen," he said at last. His eyes flicked from the table to Igneus's face. "The energy that escaped her body—we never told the council about it. That she must have been a witch. And somehow, Decimus already knew."

Igneus frowned, the gears in his artificial eye clicking softly. "You're certain?"

Neel nodded. "Completely."

Igneus's expression darkened, the lines on his face deepening. "Let me look into it," he murmured. "But until we know what she knows, this stays between us. Not a word to anyone—that also means your sister. The island's too fragile for another villain."

He turned toward the door, the light from the hall catching the faint red gleam of his eye. "Understood?"

Neel swallowed. "Understood."

Without another word, Igneus pushed the door open and vanished into the corridor, his footsteps fading into the skeletal castle's emptiness. Neel remained standing, his jaw tight and his mind churning.

Far from the fortress, beyond the reach of the council's torches and the sound of rebuilding, stood the forest. Few dared to look upon it now. Even the wind seemed to avoid it. Beneath its shadow lay the Ele family tree, the earth freshly grown over Valcom's grave.

Valcom felt both warm and cold. Death, he realized, was strangely comfortable. Heavy, but gentle—like a quilt pressing him into the earth. He could feel the dark weight around him, hear his own thoughts echo like whispers in a cavern.

Would he see his brother and his wife? His parents?

He tried to dismiss the thought, but it clung to him. Is this heaven? Then where is the Maker? Is this hell? Or something in between?

He decided to pass the time. He thought of his funeral—or what must have been a lack thereof. *You weren't yourself,* he pondered. *You were wretched. You deserved this.*

The darkness then began to shift. The weight began to lift, drawn away as if by invisible hands. A faint scratching sound reached his ears, growing louder until it clawed against his mind. The force of the soil broke.

Brilliant, blue, searing light spilled in from above.

Through the radiance, a face appeared: a woman with silver-and-gold hair that shimmered like starlight. Her round, pinkish-red face glowed with warmth, freckles scattered across her cheeks like dust from another world.

"Come," she said softly, her voice gentle but firm. She extended a freckled hand through the brilliance. "We need to have a conversation."

Valcom hesitated, staring at the hand, at the light, the promise, the unknown. Then, slowly, he reached up.

The darkness shuddered and fell away.